RETURN TO DEVIL TOWN

wayne hixon

GRINDHOUSE PRESS

Published by Grindhouse Press
POB 292644
Dayton, OH 45429
www.grindhousepress.com

Return to Devil Town: Vampires in Devil Town Book Three
Grindhouse Press #012
ISBN-13: 978-0-9849692-7-2
ISBN-10: 0984969276
Copyright © 2012 by Wayne Hixon. All rights reserved.

This book is a work of fiction.

Grindhouse Press logo copyright © 2012 by Brandon Duncan
www.corporatedemon.com

No part of this book may be reproduced, stored in a retrieval system, or transmitted by any means without the written permission of the author or publisher.

Also by Wayne Hixon

Vampires in Devil Town

Bright Black Moon (Vampires in Devil Town Book Two)

Return

to

Devil Town

One

The girl he'd met in Bunk's sat in the passenger seat of his Ford. She was hot as hell but he was starting to think there was something wrong with her. All self-deprecation aside, there *had* to be something wrong with her just to get in the car with him. For one thing, he was way too drunk to be driving. Chet usually did okay at Bunk's and a few of the redneck bars in Dayton, but this girl was way out of his league, not to mention his age bracket. Chet was just over forty and this girl didn't look like she could be out of college yet. He probably had kids running around somewhere older than her.

He started talking and realized the radio was up way too loud.

He took it down a few notches.

"Where did you say we was goin again?"

Her eyes were almost closed. Her head rested against the window.

She opened her eyes wider and looked at him. "I thought we were going back to your place."

"I'm afraid that's not going to work." He still lived with his parents and this was a sore point with him and problematic to a lot of the girls he picked up. "I'm having my house fumigated."

"Are you staying in a hotel?"

A motel would have been a really good idea and he would have actually tried to pay for a nicer one than he was used to, seeing this girl was nicer looking than ones he was used to, but after picking up both bar tabs, he was broke. He barely had enough for another pack of cigarettes. Hopefully, they'd think of something soon so he wouldn't have to put any more gas in the truck to get home.

"I'm staying tonight with a friend. He's got a wife and kids. Probably wouldn't like me bringing strangers around them."

Her eyes were closed again. She probably wasn't even listening to him. Maybe he should just pull off onto one of the mostly abandoned roads and tell her she could fuck him or walk home. Nah. She wouldn't have to fuck him, but she'd at least have to give him a blowjob.

"What about you?" he asked. "You got a place around here?"

She didn't answer. Probably passed out. That might make his plans that much easier. It wouldn't be the first time he'd mistaken rape for a night of passion.

He reached his hand out and tapped her knee.

"Hey."

He wasn't really sure he *wanted* her to wake up. His backup plan was starting to seem more appealing anyway.

He tapped her knee again. This time it wasn't so much of a tap as just contact. He left his hand there. Her jeans were skin tight. Ever since first seeing her in the bar he'd fantasized about pulling them off her. Hadn't thought it would actually happen, though. Her tits could have been bigger but beggars couldn't be choosers. Not that he had to beg. Unless buying five shots of watermelon patch was considered begging. He almost smiled. No wonder she was having trouble keeping her eyes open. He let his hand travel up her thigh. It didn't have far to travel. Her thigh wasn't much bigger than his hand.

Headed for the promised land, he thought.

He was already heading away from town, deeper into farm country. He turned off the Lynchville-Dayton Pike. A couple more turns and he would be where he wanted to be. Suchling Road. It was one of those areas nobody wanted anything to do with, just some abandoned farmhouses and woods and worthless rocky fields left to go fallow. Consequently, it had given rise to the usual rumors about Satan worshippers and vampires and all that shit.

Of course, around here, it was all blamed on the Devils.

Even just this far from the street lamps seemed more secluded.

And that made Chet feel braver.

He found the button to her jeans and popped it, wondered if she was wearing underwear. He didn't see how they could fit between her jeans and her skin.

No underwear.

He unzipped her jeans to give his hand some room to move.

He didn't feel any hair, either. That was always a turn on.

"You like that?"

Her voice startled him. He didn't pull his hand away. He found what he was looking for and slid his finger against her clitoris. She was pretty wet. Enough booze seemed to have that effect on a lot of girls.

"Do you?" he said.

"Mm-hmm."

Booze also made a lot of otherwise rational females overly susceptible to the power of suggestion. "Babe, I'm thinking I should just pull this truck over and fuck you right here."

He moved his middle finger down, into her. She was tight. He didn't want to loosen her up too much. She scooted down a little on the seat, moved her hips against his hand.

"Keep doing that and you won't need to."

He laughed. "Oh, baby, believe me, I'll need to."

"We could just go to my place."

He thought they'd already had this conversation but remembered that she had been unconscious. Luckily, the booze made him more patient. "Hmmm, and where do you live at, baby?" He wouldn't have to keep calling her baby if he could remember her name. He didn't know if she'd told him.

"It's around here. You know where Suchling Road is?"

His finger stopped mid-thrust. "Uh, yeah. You sure your house is on Suchling?" Maybe it was a longer road than he knew. Maybe people actually lived there in some other town.

"Just moved there." She pushed her hips against his hand. He resumed thrusting. "It's a fixer upper."

Now he *knew* something was wrong with her. No one would live on Suchling Road. It would be easier to tear any houses that were there down and rebuild over them. It also occurred to him that this girl wasn't old enough to own a house, regardless of the price. Suddenly, there were a lot of questions he wanted to ask her but probably wouldn't. He tried to return his focus to the road and her pussy. It wasn't really all that hard.

One-handed, he pulled the truck onto Suchling.

Woods lined each side of the road and he slowed down a little, not wanting to hit a deer. Then he figured to hell with it and accelerated. The girl's scent was starting to fill the cab, not at all unpleasing, his dick was rock hard in his pants, and he wanted to get there before this bitch figured out what a loser he was.

Up on the right was a narrow driveway that had at one time probably been gravel but was now more grass and weeds. He slowed down.

"This one?" he asked.

"Uh, yeah."

He pulled his finger from between her legs and put it in his mouth, sucked her moisture off, smelled her even more strongly.

"You don't sound too sure of yourself."

"It is. Okay so I don't really own it. I'm not really fixing it up. But it's a good place to come and party with the other kids from the school."

The school? he thought. It was possible she was talking about

Dunham College but it was a really small, really prestigious school and, having lived in Lynchville his entire life, he hadn't really heard about the students being known for their partying.

She zipped up her pants, not bothering to button them. A good sign, he thought.

"The school, huh?" He turned his high beams on and navigated the driveway slowly, not wanting a pothole or something else to knock out one of his tires.

She smiled and it looked kind of evil. "Yeah," she laughed. "The high school. That doesn't bother you, does it?"

He thought about this, but not a lot. He *thought* the age of consent was sixteen, but he didn't know for sure. If that was the case, he would be in more trouble for buying her booze than he would be for fucking her. And he'd already touched her in ways that were not exactly appropriate.

He threw his arms up and laughed. "It doesn't really matter now, does it?"

"That's the spirit."

He pulled the truck to a stop in front of the house. The girl didn't seem nearly as wasted as she did before. And now it seemed like she was the aggressor. Chet found it all hot as hell. She opened the door and hopped out.

He opened his door and she told him to leave the lights on. He started to tell her it would run the battery down until he realized *why* she probably wanted him to leave the lights on. He hopped out and slammed the door. She stood on the sagging porch, bathed in the bright halogen glow.

He puffed out his chest, sucked in his gut, and walked toward her.

His dick was still hard. He could still smell her in his nostrils. He could hear his breathing and his heart pounding in his ears. Despite all this, along with the fact that he was well over 200 pounds and the very definition of 'red-blooded male', he felt uneasy as he drew closer to the house. Maybe it was just the booze catching up to him. That would have been strange. He hadn't gotten sick from drinking since he'd been in high school and he was sure to let the girl outpace him at the bar. Maybe it was the chicken wings from Chef Uncle's ...

Still, in the truck on the way out here, he had fantasized about taking slow advantage of this wasted teenager. Now he felt like he just wanted to get it over with. Fuck her and go.

He reached the porch, wishing he didn't feel the way he did. He didn't even feel like asking her if he could film a bit of it with his phone.

He grabbed her around the hips and pulled her toward him. Her hand went to his cock. She moved in to whisper into his ear. "I really do like sex. I really do."

He reached a hand up and closed it around her breast.

"But I'm saving myself for the right person."

Huh? he thought.

"I'm sure maybe you had someone who you thought was the right person at one time. But maybe things went bad."

He pulled away from her and tried to study her expression to see if she was serious.

He heard a door to the house open and more than one set of footsteps.

The bitch smiled.

He heard laughter and he tried to scream but couldn't. He looked down and saw that the front of his shirt was red. He coughed and a spray of blood covered the bitch's face. Her smiling white teeth, droplets clinging to her hair. He turned to run but his whole body felt numb and he tumbled down the stairs, landing in a rubbery heap. He looked up and tried to find the moon but the black sky was filled with young, smiling faces.

Two

John opened the door on what he had started calling simply, "The Offering." A bucket of blood with a note that said: FOR YOU in goopy-looking letters probably written in the blood from the bucket. This was the third such offering and he'd grown a little more nervous with each one.

It meant someone besides he and Cassie knew. Which was saying a lot since *they* weren't even sure what they knew.

The suspicion had been there ever since the disappearance of John's parents a little over a year ago. Of course it wasn't a disappearance and John had been as honest with the police as he could without telling them the whole truth. And what did it matter? The truth was even more unbelievable than the thought that his parents had just dropped off the face of the planet.

But unbelievable seemed to go hand in hand with daily life in Lynchville.

It was nearly sundown. John found himself sleeping later and later these days.

He shut the door on the offering and went back into the house. There wasn't anything he could do about it. He and Cassie had developed sort of a protocol for this. He didn't have a working phone. So he waited until she came over when she got off from her job at Fink's grocery store. Then she would call Chief Bowsman with her cell. He'd come over and claim the bucket and note as "evidence" and they'd never hear anything about it again.

John was mainly baffled by the offering. Sure, he could use the blood. Had developed quite a taste for it. But it had to be living blood. A bucket of old stale blood wasn't going to do anything for him. So whoever thought they were helping him wasn't really helping him at all. That meant they didn't know what they were doing. That proved his initial theory of entrapment incorrect. He still felt hunted by the Devils, probably always would. Maybe *hunted* wasn't the right word since he was practically a Devil himself now. So it definitely wasn't one of them trying to draw him out. He'd never *really* suspected them anyway. No, he'd originally thought it was either law enforcement or one of the few rogue "vampire hunters" who had decided to start practicing in the area. But he'd ruled this out, as well. The law enforcement, i.e. people like Chief Bowsman, were far too lazy to deal with this kind of thing. It was something they didn't understand and to start investigating it would lead to a never ending trail of paperwork. Not to mention the fact that they were probably as susceptible to whatever thought control the Devils had over the town as everyone. How else could anyone decide Lynchville was a good place to raise a family despite all the disappearances, rumors, and blatant violence?

Which meant it was probably teenagers. John was only a couple years out of high school himself so it wasn't like there was some generation gap he didn't understand but if it *were* teenagers he didn't see the point. Cassie said they were kids who wanted him to turn them. John thought it was probably jocks taunting him. In the end, given the fact Cassie was still *in* high school, he chose to believe her.

That's why they decided to call it an offering.

It still didn't mean John understood it.

And it still didn't quench his need for blood.

He didn't need much.

Just a little.

He glanced at the clock, one of the few household things he hadn't given Cassie to list online. She wouldn't be there for at least another three hours.

His stomach growled.

There wasn't any food in the house.

There never was.

Three

Wayne Hixon pulled into Lynchville just after sundown. Seemed appropriate. It was a nice summer evening. He was hoping to get to the b and b *before* sundown so he could walk around and reacquaint himself with the scant downtown. Not that it really mattered. Going for a walk in the dark was probably more fitting.

He parked his car on the street, left his bags in the trunk, and went to check in. The clerk, who was probably also the owner, didn't exclaim, "Oh, you're Wayne Hixon! You wrote *Vampires in Devil Town!*" At this point, no one ever had. He didn't think they ever would. The last time he'd heard from his publisher, a reclusive dick currently on safari in Africa, he'd been told his book had sold under a hundred copies although the *digital* version was picking up steam ... priced at the never-going-to-retire-on-this price of 99 cents.

Hence the depression.

Probably hence the divorce.

Hence here he was back in Lynchville.

He was hoping Illinois would be far enough away but it wasn't. He wondered if everyone who left Lynchville had their lives become flaming wrecks when they left.

"Any place where I can grab a bite to eat?" It was nearly ten. Most things in Lynchville closed early.

The clerk looked like one giant wrinkle wearing a thinning gray perm. Wayne didn't think this question seemed wacky, but it took her a *really* long time to come up with anything. He felt like grabbing and shaking her. He wanted to listen to the sweet harmony of her slapping jowls.

"There's Chef Uncle's."

"Always has been."

Now she was actually pulling out the slender phonebook.

Wayne pulled out his phone. Contrary to his author biography, he did own a phone ... and a television and he loved and used both of them with great frequency. Well, he used to own a TV. Now he didn't really own much of anything.

Before she had even made it to the restaurant section he'd already scrolled through the listings on his phone.

The clerk was pulling on reading glasses when he leaned across the counter and said, "No. No there are not any other places besides Chef Uncle's unless I'd like to get a pizza delivered."

The woman closed the phonebook and took a deep breath. She looked like she was ready to cry. She silently pointed to a placard on the desk that said: WE RESERVE THE RIGHT TO REFUSE SERVICE.

"What?" Wayne said. "What's that mean?" He pulled his wallet out and put his Visa on the counter.

The woman looked at it and shook her head.

"Are you fucking serious?" he asked.

She picked up the phone and, for a second, Wayne thought she was calling the police but then he figured it was probably just her husband or son or something.

"We've got a problem customer."

Wayne snatched the phone out of her hand. "No," he said. "No we don't. The problem customer's leaving."

He fought the urge to bludgeon the woman with the phone and simply placed it on the counter. He smiled broadly, tipped the brim of a hat he wasn't wearing, and said, "G'day, ma'am," before kicking the door open and bursting out into the warm night.

He wanted blood.

Maybe he would go see his parents after all.

Four

John was a reader. And he enjoyed just sitting around and thinking about things. Most people would have said he seemed perpetually bored. He used to have quite a few books, records, CDs, and comic books, only some of which had been left behind by his parents. Those had long ago been given to Cassie to sell. After his initial purge, he'd bought an e-reader. Now Cassie pirated things for him and put them on a thumb drive. He couldn't afford an internet connection and so couldn't really see the point in owning a computer.

He heard the front door and hoped it was Cassie.

"Hellooo!" she called.

"In here."

He lay on the couch where he spent a good amount of time. He'd gone for another short walk today, venturing a little farther out, but had ended up right back on the couch.

"Hey there." Cassie smiled. These days, it was looking more pitying than glad to see him. Maybe she was just depressed out of her skull.

"Hey."

She carried a plastic container of salad she'd probably picked up at the deli at work. She tapped his feet, meaning he should sit up and give her room. She sat down beside him, rested the container on her lap. She was still in her uniform—khaki pants and green golf shirt, hair pulled back into a ponytail. He liked it.

She opened the container and the little cellophane sleeve containing a napkin and plastic wear.

"How was work?" he asked.

"Oh, you know. The same."

As though the small talk were destroying her, she pulled the short sleeve of her right arm up to her shoulder.

"Thank you."

She rolled her eyes. "I guess I just figured we should eat at the same time."

She took a bite of her sad little salad. He pulled a scalpel from the couch cushions. He wasn't strong enough for his fangs to come in yet and if he just tried biting her, it would be grisly. He made small cuts on her and drank just enough to satisfy himself. He tried to keep the cuts in discrete locations but, since Cassie was a seventeen-year-old girl, there were fewer and fewer places that could be dubbed discrete.

They'd been doing this for about a year. At first, they'd made a kind of game out of it. Usually it was part of their foreplay. Whenever she was on her period, she'd just spread her legs and let him do his thing. She'd at least pretended to enjoy it. Of course they'd been living with her parents at the time. It wasn't as much of an effort to come to him. Her parents had thrown him out after her father had walked in on them fucking. John was sure the only reason he still had all of his teeth was because her dad felt sorry for him.

Now Cassie just ate her salad while John suckled at her upper arm like some kind of grotesque infant. Occasionally she would bat at him and say, "Too hard."

Since there wasn't a TV and the sex had tapered off, there was a lot of empty space to fill. Cassie wasn't allowed to stay past midnight and her arrival time had gotten later and later, minimizing their time together.

She stared around the mostly empty living room.

"You saw it, didn't you?"

"The offering?" She took another bite of salad.

"Yeah."

"Do I have to call and talk to the police again?"

He took his head away from her skin. "You probably should. I mean, I can call, if you want me to."

"I'll do it in a few."

"Thanks." He turned his attention back to her arm. He kind of wanted her, so he tried to put some amount of sensuality into it but she either wasn't picking up on it or didn't care.

"Why don't you just sell this place? You could probably make enough to rent an apartment downtown for years. Then you'd be closer."

"I can't sell it until Mom and Dad are legally declared dead. Besides, it's not really that far away from you. It's even closer to the store. You would have practically passed right by me if you'd just gone home."

"It feels like it's really out of the way. Soon you're going to run out of stuff to sell. Then ..."

"Then I'll get a job."

She laughed a little, almost choked on her lettuce.

"What do you want me to say?"

She pushed his head away and closed the lid on her salad. Tugged her shirt sleeve down and put the salad on the floor.

"What? Did I do something wrong?"

She looked like she was about the cry. "No. You didn't do *any*thing. That's my point. You never *do* anything."

"So what should I do? Help me out here, Cassie. I don't exactly have a 'normal' person's perspective on things."

"I don't know. It just feels like you're ... prolonging the

inevitable."

"What's inevitable? That I become one of *them*?"

She sighed, licked her lips, sat back on the couch completely resigned. "You already *are*."

"I refuse to believe that."

"Okay. Maybe I should have added delusional to prolonging the inevitable."

"Delusional?"

She held up her hand and began ticking off on her fingers. "You don't eat people food. You sleep all day."

"Not *all* day."

She rolled her eyes. "You don't leave the house."

"I leave the house. Today I went like ... really far."

She shook her head. "You drink my blood and that keeps you alive." She quit ticking off her fingers and just threw her hands out in front of her. "You drink my blood to live. That makes you a vampire. That makes you one of them."

"Well that's because we sold the fridge and the stove on Craigslist."

Cassie gritted her teeth. "That's *why* we sold them on Craigslist."

"Okay, I was just kidding." John stood up. He had more energy now. "But you're being defeatist."

"If I were being defeatist, I would have quit this scene a long time ago."

"Quit this scene? Who talks like that?"

"*Left*. Okay? I would have *left* a long time ago."

"You're ignoring the facts."

She lay down and sprawled out on the couch, now exhausted as well as resigned. She closed her eyes. "What are the facts, John?"

"That woman and her thugs bit me and I changed. You remember that, don't you? That time when I killed my parents and one of my dad's best friends and that boy who wanted to do dirty things to you. Remember that? Just a little more than a year ago. Oh yeah, I almost killed you, too. I remember it pretty well."

"Okay, yes, I remember it. You don't have to shout."

"I'm not shouting."

"You're talking really loud then. So they bit you and you changed. Now you're one of them so ... what am I missing?"

"I drink your blood every time you come over and you haven't changed."

"But you don't bite me."

"Because I don't have fangs because I'm not one of them."

"But I think you *are*." She reached out and patted his leg. "I think you're just a pup and I think you drink only enough blood to keep you alive so you're never strong enough to be like they were. Or are. Or whatever."

"But I was. Why did it reverse when we killed that bitch?"

"Because you were directly under their influence. You were devouring a person a night. You had *fuel*."

He threw his arms out to his sides. "So what should I do? We're back to square one."

Cassie sat up and swung her legs onto the floor. "Also, we don't know that we killed that woman. We know she wasn't the only one. We only closed one of the doors. Your brother said that all of Lynchville was a door."

"It's still debatable that you actually had that conversation."

This time she punched him on the leg.

"Ow. So okay. What now?"

She moved close to him and pecked him on the cheek. "So now I think you need to decide if you want to join real society or if you want to admit that you're one of them and start behaving appropriately."

"Appropriately?"

She chomped her teeth at him.

"Oh no," he said. "I'm not doing that."

"Then don't do anything and see what happens."

"I'm not killing people, Cassie."

She dramatically pounded her fists lightly against his chest. "But you're *killing me*." It was as close to playful as she'd been all night. "Besides, *you* wouldn't have to kill anyone. You have a whole gaggle of teenagers ready to do your bidding."

"How do you know that?"

"I have my suspicions."

"Maybe you should tell Bowsman that when you call?"

"I'm waiting to read the obituaries in the paper. But I will call on my way out ... Which is now, I think."

"*Cassie.*"

"*John.* I think I'm done for the night. I'm tired and I have school tomorrow. Besides, you got what you needed."

I *need* company, he thought. But he wouldn't say that. More specifically, he thought he needed *her* company but it had been so long since he'd talked to anyone except her or Bowsman that he couldn't even really say anymore.

Five

Wayne pulled up in front of the farmhouse. His parking job was shoddy and his blood was up. In fact, he *had* stopped at Chef Uncle's. He was hoping he could goad some local redneck into a fight but the only people in there were a couple of harmless old drunks and some gross skanks who were taking turns snorting pills in the bathroom. He'd had a few shots of Jack and a couple of Buds and decided that was the least he needed to face his parents.

Maybe it was just his wounded pride that had him so riled up.

Yes, he'd written a book and gotten it published and that was something to be proud of. But that pride had dissipated nearly the second he'd received his first royalty check. Everything else was just icing on the humiliation cake he'd baked for himself.

The reason he was back in Lynchville wasn't any type of reunion or homecoming. His marriage had slowly unraveled and, just yesterday, he'd signed the divorce papers and attended the hearing in the same day. He hadn't lived with Alison and Major for the past six months. He'd lived in an apartment that he'd barely been able to make the rent on. And now that the divorce was finalized, he'd be expected to cough up child support for Major. He was happy to do that but he couldn't do that and continue to pay rent for himself. Not on the instructor salary he was getting in Illinois. So he'd looked at colleges around his parents. Even a part time gig at Dunham was more than he was used to making. And there were a couple of community colleges in the area. Maybe he could continue working on his doctorate and eventually become an adult who was able to provide for himself *and* his family.

Of course, he'd neglected to tell his parents about any of this. His mother called every couple of weeks mostly because she was sad and lonely. His father never listened to her and she just wanted someone to talk at. Wayne usually just told her he was fine and handed the phone off to Major as quickly as possible.

He wasn't nervous or anything. It had taken him thirty-five years, but he was sure his mom and dad were both waiting for him to fail miserably and he felt it was his birth right for them to put him up when he needed it. He would pay with the pain of being around them that many hours a day.

Maybe he'd have to hit up Chef Uncle's more often, try and find a skank who didn't make him want to vomit to take him in.

He popped the trunk and turned off the engine. He got out, went to the trunk, and grabbed his suitcase and the two boxes he had his belongings in. His relative laze coupled with the space of the car and the inevitably small confines of whatever hellhole he would potentially inhabit gave him the ability to edit his possessions with rabid ferocity. He burned his manuscripts, donated most of his clothes, and simply walked out on everything else. Let Alison deal with it. He was done. He had a couple changes of clothes, his laptop, mp3 player, and phone. If he could, he would have Major too. But everything else was superfluous.

Standing on the porch, he thought he could probably just walk right in but liked the idea of pounding on the door and ringing the bell at midnight even better.

So he stood there in front of his boxes and waited. They'd probably been asleep for a few hours so he thought he would give them a few minutes to clear their rotten heads and come down and open the door for him. He called his mom "Old Bitch" and his dad "Dick," even though his name was Robert, and had ever since he was a teenager. They took it like the troopers they were.

Still no answer.

Odd.

He looked back at the driveway to make sure their cars were still there. His father was always threatening to retire to Florida and they took a lot of vacations.

Both cars were still there.

Wayne nudged the boxes to the side and opened the door. The door fell off its hinges and came to lean against his shoulder.

Had he not had a few drinks in him, he would have probably immediately bolted for the car and tried to figure out what had happened later. But with this liquid courage flowing through him and his anger not reduced in the least, he put one foot up on his box and bellowed into the house.

"Hello!?"

They obviously weren't in there. It was stupid of him to even bother yelling. An attempt to look into the house made him remember how dark it was out here in the middle of nowhere.

He accessed a flashlight app on his phone and shined it into the house. The damage his cursory glance revealed made him rethink his approach to the house.

He turned and walked off the porch, stopped in the yard, and turned to look at the house.

He didn't know if it was the dark or his familiarity with the house but he'd overlooked something.

The house had been burned.

Most of the roof was gone. Black smudges bloomed around the broken windows.

Hm, he thought.

This had to have happened within the last couple of weeks. If his parents had a cell phone he would have tried to call it. But they only had a landline.

Even as he thought it was a stupid idea, he pulled their information and pressed the call icon.

He didn't hear it ring within the house.

Standing there in the yard of his ruined childhood home, he didn't know what to do.

He guessed he would call the police.

He got the number from Google and called.

"Lynchville Police. This is Earl. How may I help you?"

"Hi, uh, Earl. My name's Wayne Hixon and—"

"Ah, there you are."

"Here I am." That wasn't exactly the response he was expecting. He thought he would have to do a bit more explaining.

"You should probably come down to the station."

"I'm looking for my parents. Do you know if they're okay?"

"You'd better come to the station, Mr. Hixon."

Not okay, he thought. Having grown up surrounded by the people of Lynchville, *being* a person (at least formerly) of Lynchville, he knew not to press the issue with the deputy or the receptionist or whatever Earl was or it would just make him retreat into his shell.

"I'll be there in a few minutes."

"You know where it is?"

"Yeah, I know where it is." He'd been there a couple of times during his teenage years. He ended the call, retrieved his suitcase and boxes, and put them back in his car.

Six

There was a pounding on the door. Probably Bowsman.

John crossed the living room and opened his door. Bowsman wasn't even wearing his uniform. He was barely wearing clothes. Just swim trunks, a towel slung over his shoulders, and a pair of flip flops.

"Sorry about this." He motioned down to all of his exposed girth. "I just came from the swim club."

"Sorry about this." John motioned down to the bucket of blood.

Chief Bowsman looked at it.

"You're doing the right thing. That's why I'm handling this case special."

"I really appreciate it."

"Just don't want anybody botching things up."

"Have you made any progress so far?"

"About?"

"The blood. My parents." *The violence? The disappearances? The mysterious deaths?* "Anything?"

"I think your parents are somewhere in the town. Probably dead, but still here. We'll find them. The blood? It has me at a bit of a loss."

"Have you analyzed it or anything?"

"Oh, uh huh."

John figured he probably hadn't. "And was it human blood or animal blood? Something else?"

"I'm afraid I can't release that information at this time."

It's because you don't fucking know, John thought.

"As soon as I know anything about either your parents or the blood, I'll give you a call."

"I don't have a phone."

"I'll give Cathy a call."

"Cassie."

"Yep. Sweet girl."

"The best."

"I guess I'd better get this cleaned up and tagged. Photographed."

"I'll leave you to it. Hopefully this will be the last time you have to come out."

"Hopefully."

John shut the door. He went into the kitchen and parted the blinds just enough so he could see Bowsman. He dumped the blood over the porch and shook the bucket until it stopped dripping. He almost walked off without the note, stopped and turned around, and came back for it. He crumpled it up and put it into the pocket of his swim trunks.

John thought maybe he should let Bowsman know he was watching him but he didn't think that would engender him to the man at all. John figured the buckets were probably just filled with animal blood and were really no more than a nuisance for him. But he knew Bowsman thought he was guilty of killing his parents and, provided Bowsman *was* looking into the case, John didn't want to give his suspicions any more cause.

He went back to the couch to pick up the Murakami book he was reading but he was having a hard time concentrating. It wasn't the brief encounter with Bowsman. Over the past year he'd had a number of similarly laconic, equally disinterested meetings with the Chief. First dealing with his parents and now the offerings. It also wasn't just Cassie's abrupt departure. It certainly wasn't the first, but it *had* been happening with more frequency. That bothered him but he didn't know what he was supposed to do about it. He loved her and was closer to her than he had been with anyone. But she was the first person he'd ever had sex with, they'd gone through a horribly traumatic event together and ... well, things had been unraveling ever since. She was only seventeen. At this point in her life, she should be having fun and looking forward to going away to college. He was a burden. It seemed inevitable. He could only do what he was able, which wasn't very much.

That was what was bothering him.

She'd told him he didn't do anything.

She was probably right.

Maybe he was just avoiding the inevitable. About everything.

But he was taking some small steps.

Each day he'd been going for walks, a little farther each time. Ideally he was going to try walking out of Lynchville. He had a feeling he wouldn't be able to. He supposed he could just have Cassie drive him out, but he was afraid of what it might do to him, to leave that fast if the town really wanted to keep hold of him. He might be dead before Cassie even realized what was happening to him. He could do it himself but he'd sold his car. If he asked to borrow Cassie's, she'd ask to come with him.

His original plan was the best. That way he'd be alone. More and more, and maybe it was just the *constant* loneliness, he enjoyed doing things alone.

Maybe he was a freak.

Maybe he needed to find someone like him.

He wondered if Cassie would let him make her like him.

She would if she loved him, he thought.

Seven

Wayne sat in the reception area, reeling. The only reason he was still at the station was because Earl, who was actually a deputy, told him that if he left he would cite him for public intoxication. That was after telling him both of his parents died in the housefire two weeks ago. If Wayne had been in Earl's place, he would have seen it as preventative maintenance.

Of course, Wayne assumed it was probably more his belligerence than drunkenness as the reason he was sitting here. He had just wanted some very basic questions answered.

How long ago had this happened?

Why wasn't he notified?

Were they buried yet?

Why wasn't he notified?

Why did Earl have such a fat red neck?

Why wasn't he fucking notified?

Why was everyone in this town such an inbred moron?

After handcuffing Wayne to the chair, Earl had explained things to him.

"It's not up to us to notify all the family members. In the case of an emergency, we contact the closest family member. In this case, that was your Aunt Beulah."

"Fucking whore," Wayne growled.

"I found her quite pleasant. She said you hadn't been back in town for over a decade. Said you had a wife and a son and everything and never even brought them to see your ma and pa."

"They could have come to me just as easily. I wasn't even a day away."

"Well, with most everything in the house gone and you doing your best to avoid creditors, no one knew where to find you. She even bought a copy of that book you wrote."

"*Vampires in Devil Town?*" Great, he thought, and mentally deducted one copy from his sales figures. If it wasn't bought to read, it didn't count.

"That's the one. The one about Lynchville."

"The town's called Lynchville. It's just a trashy vampire novel. It doesn't have anything to do with this shitburg."

"Hm. Some people might not feel that way."

Earl continued talking but Wayne's mind had begun wandering.

"She thought she got lucky when she found your publisher's address in the front of the book."

Some might not feel that way. Was that a threat?

"She sent the editor a letter. Last I heard, she hasn't heard back."

Was it possible his parents had died because of some schlock book he'd written?

"That's just bad customer service if you ask me. Publisher's in Dayton. What's it take her letter to get there? One day. Two, tops. Seems like he would have gotten in touch with her or, maybe even, *you.*"

"He's on safari in fucking *Africa!*"

Earl kept talking.

Wayne pulled himself into the closest thing he could come to the fetal position while handcuffed to a not extremely comfortable chair and waited hopefully for the apocalypse.

Eight

"I'm in front of your house." Cassie hit END as soon as she said this.

A few seconds later, Melanie came bounding out of the house. She opened the passenger door and slid into the seat. "Hi, sister."

"Hey."

"Where to?"

"I need to go home and get out of these clothes. Maybe grab a shower."

"Then we don't really need to go anywhere. I can just tell my parents I'm sleeping over."

"Sure." Cassie smiled. "I'm sure it'll be okay with my folks. It's probably a plus that you don't have a dick."

"Nope. That I do not."

Cassie reached across the seat and poked Melanie in the crotch. "You have a magic button."

Melanie made a sound that was half-squeal/half-moan and said, "I have more than one."

"Me too." Cassie backed out of the driveway. They were only a couple of minutes from her house.

Melanie leaned across the seat and took Cassie's earlobe into her mouth. "Is this one?"

"Mm-hmm."

Melanie ran her tongue down the side of Cassie's neck. "What about this?"

"Mm-hmm."

"I think you might have a few more."

"Probably."

"Did you talk to John?"

"I will."

"Did you fuck him?"

"No. *Relax*. Jealousy isn't becoming. And you knew I was doing that with him before we started doing anything."

"Not jealousy. Curiosity."

"Oh yeah?"

"Sure. Who wouldn't be?"

"What do you mean?"

"Well, he's a Devil isn't he?"

"Jesus. Does everyone know that?"

Melanie paused for a second. "Um, yeah, I think so."

"How?"

"It's a small town, Cass."

"Still ... I thought he and I were the only ones who knew. Actually, I'm not even sure *he* knows. Or he's in denial or something."

"He has to know."

"Wait, now I'm not sure what you're talking about."

"I'm talking about us. John being a Devil. Everything. He has to know."

"He will. Just let me do it my way. Also, if you really are curious about ... you know, I wouldn't mind sharing."

Melanie laughed but it seemed loaded. Like maybe she really would think about it.

Cassie turned onto Maple and sped to her house, pulling past her dad's Mercedes and parking next to her mom's Volvo.

Before going inside, Cassie said, "So, what do you think? I know you were thinking about it."

"Hm. Let me keep thinking about it."

"Okay."

"I guess I'm not really that surprised that you wouldn't mind sharing *him*, but what about me?"

"The biology's all different. He has an outie and you have an innie."

"So?"

"Look. I love you both but you make me feel things he couldn't in a million years. There. Does that make you feel better?"

"As long as it's not just something you're saying."

"It's not. Promise. You'll get to see how you make me feel veddy veddy soon."

Cassie unlocked the door and they went inside, just a couple of giggling high school girls.

Nine

Ilya had found her current body in a drab apartment outside of Omaha, Nebraska. She had walked this earth longer than anyone and had kept her original body longer than any of her kind but those kids had seen to its destruction. The shame had driven her farther from Lynchville than she'd ever been. She had inhabited several bodies during that time period and she had learned a few things.

Each body was different. Capable only of what the previous inhabitant was capable of. This, she thought, must be what it was like for most of her kind. If it wasn't craving for that sensation only living flesh could provide, she would have preferred to remain in spirit form. Coming into a new body was like learning to drive a different car. They all had their quirks. She had learned to avoid the ones who were crippled or too fat.

Also, she wasn't able to completely take over the brain. She still shared many of their wants and desires. Sometimes even their responsibilities. She had learned to avoid people with families or people who were married to their jobs.

That left people like Patrick Fishman.

He wasn't exactly thin but he wasn't too fat. He was ... nondescript. Almost the very definition of. He worked nine to five at a data entry job. She had only had to spend a few days shadowing him. He worked in a lonely cubicle where he never spoke more than to exchange the usual pleasantries with people. He sat there until five, taking an hour off to eat a peanut butter or turkey sandwich in the break room while watching the noon news. While working, he didn't listen to the radio or audio books or anything. She thought he must be completely empty on the inside. When she finally entered him, she realized she wasn't that far from the truth.

She had endured one day of him at work before finally taking control.

At work, he thought about virtually nothing. Sometimes while he entered the account numbers and payments from people's bills, he would think, "They owe a lot of money." But mostly it was just people making the minimum payments on minimal accounts. There was a lingering feeling of resentment. Sometimes there were some pleasant memories. Mostly from childhood. Mostly involving what Ilya thought was probably his family. There was no hint of female involvement. She was pretty sure Patrick had never had sex. She would see if she could change that. Of course, it wouldn't be a memory he could keep. He'd have to die if Ilya ever wanted to leave.

He left work to go back to his drab apartment in a drab part of town, usually stopping at a drive-thru restaurant to get some food to eat in front of the television. In her day of habitation and few days of shadowing she didn't even observe him masturbate.

His apartment was decorated with bland furniture and prints, almost like it was decorated through some belief that these objects needed to be there.

Once she entered, he was still there, but it was mostly a residual kind of there. Memories. Something like a conscience. Feelings. But those things began dying away the second she took up his body and, within a couple of weeks, would be gone completely. She almost wished this wasn't the case.

She was going to show him some interesting things. Probably more experiences—real, *visceral* experiences—than he'd had his entire life.

Take, for instance, the hooker on the bed.

They were in the middle of Illinois, land of truck stops, and Ilya had felt the urge crawl over her. She needed to eat. She wanted blood. Since she was in the body of a human and he would probably remain human the entire time she was with him, she could have remained alive eating the same crap he'd been shoveling in probably his entire life. But she *wanted* blood. And she felt there was more to it than simple craving. It was who she was, a drinker of blood, and she thought it kept her senses sharp.

The hooker had introduced herself as Jade. She was probably in her twenties but hadn't aged well and looked closer to forty. She was definitely on something and probably needed money to buy more so when Ilya asked her what she could get for fifty dollars, Jade had told her she could get pretty much anything she wanted.

Ilya's view of this was very liberal.

It had been several months since she'd inhabited the body of a man and she'd forgotten how much fun that could be.

The whore was thin to begin with and whatever drug she was on had further wasted her but, still, the feeling of total dominance Ilya was able to assert with Patrick's body was empowering.

Ilya had thoroughly abused every orifice on Jade's body but apparently hadn't sent up any red flags yet.

Jade was resting on the bed, not a cover or shred of clothing on her bony, scabby body.

Ilya was in the small, hot bathroom, enjoying the pungent and most likely diseased reek of sex rising from her body. Despite coming on the hooker's face, her penis was still erect.

Of course it was.

Ilya hadn't been completely satisfied yet.

She still had the itch that she couldn't reach with Patrick's body alone. Before leaving Patrick's lair of boredom, she had packed a duffel bag with some clothes, a surprising amount of cash he'd kept in a book called *The Seven Habits of Highly Effective People,* and some kitchen items. She grabbed a large butcher knife and a corkscrew, opened the bathroom door, and began walking toward the bed.

Jade stared up at the ceiling, her arms over her chest.

Ilya straddled her with Patrick's bulky body and said, "Don't be scared."

If Jade hadn't screamed, Ilya wouldn't have cut her throat first thing.

It was probably better for Jade that she did.

Ten

Wayne was starting to feel like the sole participant in his staring contest with Earl when Chief Bowsman arrived just after dawn.

"Hey Chief, where are the donuts!"

"Who's this?"

"That's Wayne Hixon. You know, the son of the couple whose house ..."

"And," Wayne shouted, "author of *Vampires in Devil Town*! The book that's going to bring down Lynchville!"

Bowsman fiddled with some keys attached to a retractable belt device. He unlocked the handcuffs and said, "People would have to read it in order for that to happen."

Wayne rubbed his wrist and stood up. Bowsman was a pretty large man so Wayne didn't shout as loudly when he said, "I need some questions answered."

Bowsman smiled. Wayne thought it looked like he was enjoying this. "I think you need to talk to the insurance company now. Our business with the affair is done. I don't want to see you any more."

Wayne was too tired to think of anything else to say so he said, "I don't want to see you either." He was almost out of the station before he remembered Earl had confiscated his phone. Not that there was anyone he wanted to call anyway but, provided the station had a WiFi connection, he could have spent the wee hours of the morning watching YouTube instead of Earl doing that droopy head, jello-neck kind of thing.

Wayne raised his arms up to the ceiling and, completely against his better judgment, bellowed, "CAN I PLEASE HAVE MY PHONE BACK!"

Bowsman jammed it roughly into Wayne's chest and nudged him toward the front doors.

He got in his car and drove it down the block just far enough to be out of sight from the station. His phone was dead so he had to plug it in. He guessed he could call his aunt or the insurance company but he didn't see either one of those conversations going well.

He was so tired.

He called Chef Uncle's and was surprised when someone answered the phone.

"What time do you start serving liquor?"

"Six AM."

"Fuck. Yes."

"Excuse me?"

"I just meant to say, 'God bless your soul.'"

Wayne drove the few blocks to Chef Uncle's. He walked in and ordered a Jack and Coke and "food." When the waitress asked him what kind of food he wanted he said he didn't care. He walked to the jukebox and furiously fed change into it like he was eager to divest himself of every last cent he had. He selected Blue Oyster Cult because it wasn't country and it was close to the beginning of the alphabet. He sat in a booth in the corner, guessing that "Don't Fear the Reaper" was going to be blaring for at least the next hour. He didn't really find it hilarious until other people came in and looked bemusedly around them. He wondered how many times it would play before they complained.

While he observed them, he thought about what he was going to do.

Going back to Illinois was not an option. There was a restraining order involved. Maybe he could get a job at Chef Uncle's but he still wouldn't have a place to stay. He probably had enough left on his credit card to stay at a cheap hotel for maybe a week.

Rachel.

The name came storming to him. He didn't know why he hadn't thought of her before. He'd used her name as the female protaganist in *Vampires*. She was the closest thing he'd had to a high school sweetheart, which meant they spent a few months fucking before she realized what a loser he was and he realized how boring she was. But, over the years, he'd romanticized the relationship somewhat. He'd remembered her ass being amazingly firm in his hands. Whatever. It had been over seventeen years. She was probably gross and flabby by now. But it was someone to talk to. He wasn't specifically thinking about using her for a place to stay.

He thought about looking her up online but figured she'd probably been married at least once by now and, since he still remembered her parents' phone number, he called them not minding that it was just after seven in the morning. Whatever. They were ancient by now. Probably got up with the sun.

"Hello?"

"Hi," Wayne said, using a strange, husky voice.

"Can I help you?"

"Yeah. This is Randy Michaels from the school. I'm trying to reach Rachel for some importance." He thought maybe if he just made the whole statement as vague and confusing as possible, he would overwhelm the woman and get the information.

"Sir, she hasn't lived here for years."

"I know. I had her new number on the computer but a crash happened and I lost it and now I don't have it. I'm from the school again."

"Well hold on."

Thirty seconds later he was calling Rachel.

She didn't seem to be as awake when she said, "Hello."

"Hey, Rache, it's Wayne!" He tried to sound really bright and cheerful, like a morning radio show host.

"Who?"

"Wayne Hixon! From high school!"

"Yes?"

"How ya doin?"

"Well, um, married. With kids. Three of them."

"That's a really swell number."

"Is there ... something I can help you with?"

"I was wondering if you'd like to get together sometime." He figured if she was married with three kids, then he could probably at least fuck her or get a blowjob if she'd let herself go too much.

"Um, no."

"That's it, huh? Just no?"

He thought he heard her laughing before she ended the call.

Wayne had never felt as fucked as he had at that point. The waitress brought him a sarcastic amount of food and an entire pitcher of coffee, maybe as a hint. Wayne didn't think he was hungry but he ate with gusto and ordered another beer. Maybe it was the soundtrack. His parents had never sent him a copy of the will. He assumed they had *made* a will. It would have just been irresponsible not to. He also assumed he was *in* the will, being the only child and all. He could call his aunt later and get some things worked out. In the meantime, he wondered if the plumbing in the house still worked. It was summer. The bottom part of the house seemed to be mostly there. He wouldn't need things like heat and insulation for a few months at least.

When he finished eating, he vomited all over the table and walked out.

Eleven

Cassie awoke to sunlight filling her room and the sound of birds chirping. She had a pleasant feeling. Melanie had exhausted her last night. She hoped she had returned the favor. She wasn't still in the bed with her. Cassie grabbed her phone. She had one unread text. It was Melanie saying, "woke up and went home. last nite was great." Cassie smiled. She got out of bed, pulled on a thin robe and some clean clothes and headed to the bathroom to shower off the girl come and brush the taste of Melanie from her mouth, even though she would have rather let it linger.

In the shower, she thought about "The John Problem." Melanie wasn't the only reason this issue seemed pressing. There was only another week of school left. That meant she would soon have a copious amount of time to fill. John would expect her to spend that time with him. She didn't know if she could take that. Her parents had made it clear he was no longer welcome in their house and she understood that. Which meant spending all of that free time at John's. He'd already had the power cut off for the summer. He said the only reason he needed it was for the heat. She wasn't even sure if he would need it for that by the time winter rolled around. So it wasn't even like she could take a TV over there or anything. And talking to him was increasingly difficult.

But she felt bad about just leaving him abruptly. She wondered if he would just let himself starve. She needed to find a replacement for herself. She knew the thing with her and Melanie wasn't permanent and she thought Melanie realized that too. But, for now, Cassie was happy. She wasn't sure John could *ever* be happy. She certainly wasn't the one to make him happy. But she thought he could be happier. His problem was that he was using her but felt bad for using her. He really just needed her for her blood but he'd convinced himself he enjoyed her company, that they were a couple, and needed to spend time together. What he really needed was either a mother or a slave.

That was why Cassie was determined to find out who was leaving the offerings. Whoever was doing that, and it might be more than one person, was enamored with what John had become. In exchange for John turning them, they would undoubtedly do whatever he asked them to do. Cassie had a fairly good idea who it was. She needed a little more proof before she acted on it.

This morning she was going to check the obituaries. Spend today asking some questions at school. Maybe do some following this weekend.

She dried herself off, smiling at the bruise-like hickies descending the insides of her thighs. Melanie had marked her. Despite what she had said, she was jealous as hell. She certainly couldn't let John be with her until they faded. Or maybe she could. Maybe she would. See if he had the balls to ask her about it. Maybe they could have it out then.

Maybe.

Cassie pulled on her clothes and headed downstairs. Her dad had already left for work and her mom was probably still asleep. Her dad had left the Lynchville *Chronicle* on the kitchen table next to a half-empty coffee mug and plate with crumbs on it. He was kind of a slob but, between her mother and the housekeeper who came twice a week, his messes were well-tended.

She grabbed some coffee from the pot, figuring it hadn't been brewed so long ago as to be gross, and sat at the table. She flipped to the obituary section. Lynchville was so small this wasn't a huge task to scan. The paper only came out weekly. This week there had been five deaths. She looked for a certain profile. Two of them died of cancer. Both of them were in their seventies. They were out. One had died at birth. Out. One had died of a heart attack but reading the brief write-up revealed he wasn't actually in Lynchville when he died. He was just *from* Lynchville and had died at his home in Denton, Texas. Out. The last one, however, fit her profile exactly. Chet Hendricks. Forty years old. Died in a one car accident on Route 4. The funeral would probably be closed casket because, if what she thought were true, he hadn't died in a car accident at all. But she was sure whoever had killed him and drained his blood to leave in front of John's house wanted to make the death look accidental. Smashed and beheaded probably. Something resulting in massive blood loss.

If the police deployed a crime scene investigation unit for every seemingly routine accident in Lynchville, and if those CSI units were as amazingly skilled as the ones on TV, Cassie guessed they would find a lot of things that didn't quite add up. But they didn't deploy those units for everything. She doubted a town as small as Lynchville even had one of those units. And if they did, she didn't think they would send them out anyway. Or, if they did, they would make it a point *not* to find anything out of the ordinary. Admittedly, Cassie had seen the Devils close-up so she had proof. She had reason to believe in the supernatural. But even before that event on John's farm, she knew something was fucked up in Lynchville. There was a lot of death. A lot of craziness. And a lot of blasé attitudes toward this kind of thing.

Before her encounter with the Devils, she knew something was off but she didn't necessarily believe it was supernatural. She thought the police were probably just concepts and that everyone in Lynchville had some stake in the corruption so no one said anything. But now she knew it was all the doing of the Devils. They had a way of making people do things. And not do things. They were mostly unseen and that was the way they preferred it. And not all of them stayed in Lynchville but it was a place they preferred. It contained the opening to that other world, Neverly, the town behind Lynchville.

Cassie had had a brief glimpse of that other town. The *reality* of that other town. It had chilled her.

She knew many other people had glimpsed it. A Devil could show this place to a potential victim, seducing them with it. Getting the victim to come to them.

And then, before the victim knew it, the door had closed, they were meat for the Devils, and would never be seen again.

There were very few people who could open this door to others. Provided a place had the right energy, it could be a doorway. Some people were keys to that door. She occasionally fucked one of those people.

If everything were to bubble to the surface like she thought it would, she would have to tell him this. Let him know he could get to that place. A place he could hide.

She sipped the coffee to try and give her mind focus. She was getting ahead of herself. Maybe this Neverly had a tendency to seduce her as well. She had sworn to never tell John about his power to go there. As much as she didn't want to be with him, she also didn't want to think about what would happen if he crossed over. The bloodsucking, earthbound Devils were monsters, of course, but they were also still vaguely human. The ones in that other place ... She took another sip of coffee.

She really needed to think about something else.

Something more pleasant.

Like these poseur Devils who were sacrificing people around town and how she could bring them and John together so Cassie could remember what it felt like to be free.

Twelve

Wayne tried sleeping on one of the charred couches he remembered from childhood but woke up because he thought he was suffocating and went out to sleep in his car with the windows rolled down. It was still suffocating but a different kind of suffocating. This was probably how people became homeless. He got online to check and see if there were any colleges in the area with positions available. He didn't find anything. Probably something he should have checked before coming out here. The year was practically over. Maybe listings for the next school year would start popping up soon.

If he didn't have enough money to rent a shower then he could probably find one of those interstate truck stops with the pay showers. Use a laundromat to wash his clothes.

There *was* a part of him that wanted to mourn his parents. He wasn't completely heartless, but it felt like there were too many things he had to do. Also, his life was so sad already that he didn't see the sense in grieving for something he didn't have any control over. Less than a year ago, he'd had a beautiful wife, a loving and smart son, a house in a decent suburb his in-laws had bought with cash for their precious only daughter. What he didn't have was a grasp on how tenuous all those things were. In the end, he'd come out of it with nothing except his borderline personality disorder. Of course people told him he would always have Major, but that was only true to an extent. It's a lot different to go from living with someone to seeing them every other weekend. If he ended up staying in Lynchville, it would be even less than that. Maybe a few days around Christmas. A few weeks in the summer. Anything else would be impractical. He wouldn't have the money to drive back and forth to Illinois and he couldn't see Alison willing to spend money to make it easier for her only son to spend time with a man she hated.

Wayne let out a long, shaky sigh, the kind that could turn into a sob if he let it.

He should probably call around and see if there were any job openings anywhere, even if it meant bagging groceries.

He felt like he needed to clear his head first. He contemplated going for a drive, but that would eventually mean spending money he didn't have on gas.

Maybe he would go for a walk. Given Chief Bowsman's warning and the way he'd brought the party at Chef Uncle's this morning, downtown was probably out. He had never been much of a nature person but here he was surrounded by acres and acres of growing corn and woods. He wasn't that far from the reserve. They had trails and things there.

Fuck trails, he thought.

It shouldn't really be considered nature if there were civil little trails cut through the whole thing.

No. He would plow through those woods as though they were virgin territory. He would explore until he was raped by thorns and eaten by ticks or wolves. Or maybe just until he got tired.

He walked to the edge of the yard and stepped into the woods. It felt like an absurd thing to do. Shouldn't it be a primal urge or something? Were the evolutionists as fucked in the head as the creationists?

Once in the darker confines of the woods, under the leafy canopy, he started to feel more relaxed. Maybe *relaxed* wasn't the right word. He thought maybe "at peace" was what he was looking for but dismissed that because it made him sound like a damn hippie.

But there *was* something about the smells and the sounds of the birds and the insects and the ... screaming?

Wayne was really *really* far away from being a Good Samaritan so he waited until he heard it a few more times before he began moving in that direction. He didn't have anything to defend himself or anybody else with. He wasn't sure how susceptible someone capable of evincing that kind of scream would be to a well-placed cutting remark or a firm grasp of vocabulary. He wasn't even wearing his blazer.

He felt like running would probably do more harm than good but he *did* walk considerably faster than he had been.

The scream was the kind often described as "blood curdling."

He broke into something close to a lope but didn't think a heart attack would benefit anyone so he went back to his previous pace, now with a painful stitch in his side.

"Hello!" He thought maybe announcing himself could lessen an impending crisis.

The screams continued.

He saw a house through the woods. He'd almost forgotten about that house. In all his years growing up here, he'd never mustered up the courage to go inside it. There were many such houses in Lynchville. Old farm houses that had just been abandoned. Many times people didn't even know the reasons. The residents were just never heard from again. Wayne often suspected that if someone were to ask the friendly neighborhood bank, they would probably get a much better idea. He'd even written about a house like this and maybe, somewhere in his subconscious, this was the house he'd written about.

In short, it looked exactly like the type of place screams like that would be coming from.

Stopping about twenty feet behind the house, he strained over the blood pounding in his ears to see if the screams continued.

"Hello?" he said again.

Panic must have rendered him dumb. He didn't know why he didn't think of it before but he pulled his phone from his pocket. Luckily, there was a bit of battery left. Within seconds he could call the police or, if he came face to face with the perpetrator, he could take his picture and instantly upload it to his twenty-four followers on Twitter.

He continued walking toward the house, resolving to call the police if he heard the scream again. He would walk around and look in all the windows. Even though he was older and wiser, he still had no intention of entering that house. In fact, maybe it was that wisdom that gave him more reasons *not* to enter.

He heard another sound but this time it sounded like laughter. Not mean, sadistic laughter. Light, happy laughter. He felt good about leaving on that note. After all, he hadn't *seen* anyone doing anything. Now if someone were to catch him looking in their windows, he'd just feel like a creep.

He turned to walk away from the house and back toward the woods. He had a sudden feeling of anxiety and took off running faster than he had run here. It was a feeling he hadn't had since he was a kid. His dad would send him out to the woodshed with a wheelbarrow to fetch wood. He was always fine until he turned to go back to the house. That was when the panic seized him. Sometimes he would take off running and leave the wheelbarrow behind. His dad usually told him if he didn't go back to get it, he was going to make him sleep outside in his underwear.

Reaching the woods intact, panicked and breathing heavily, he'd forgotten what that feeling was. Cautiously, he drew to a stop and looked over his shoulder at the house. He still didn't see any murder victims or comedians. No clowns, either.

Jesus, he didn't even know why he'd entertained the thought of staying in Lynchville without his parents to mooch off of.

He'd been here less than twenty-four hours and he'd already discovered his parents were dead, been threatened by the police, spent a night in jail, and been scared out of his skull.

The reality of how completely and totally he was fucked came back to him. There were probably a number of people who thought anger was just a manifestation of some deeper fear. Wayne wouldn't disagree with them. Especially now as the anger swallowed the fear in a red tidal wave and he stormed around the woods, ripping up saplings, kicking dirt clods, karate chopping trees, and shouting, "Fuck! Fuck! Fuck!" all the while.

It was probably, like, his favorite word.

Thirteen

John woke up earlier than normal. Starving, as usual. He didn't feel like reading so he opened the door to go outside and paused to look down and make sure he hadn't been left another offering. Two days in a row would have been an even greater cause for alarm. Not that he was exactly sure why he should worry about it since it didn't seem like anyone else was.

Today he thought maybe he would try to make it to the Hixon place. Since he and Cassie were once confined to this farm it seemed ironic that he now chose not to leave. He should escape as much as possible, if not permanently, just to celebrate that right. But it wasn't really that he chose not to leave. There just wasn't any place to go. There had been Cassie's and, once that was out, that was it. He knew Cassie had friends but she'd been careful to never have them around John for very long. He didn't really know her reasoning. She didn't seem jealous but, he guessed if he wanted to be kind to himself, that could have been a reason. More likely she was embarrassed of him. A twenty-year-old jobless loser. A sad sack. Quite possibly a Devil and a murderer. And with the social skills of ... what? A paper cup, maybe?

To even get to the woods, John had to walk through a large cornfield. This year, the local farming outfit hadn't planted anything in it. Come harvest, they'd have to pay royalties. Maybe they didn't know who to pay or maybe they'd rather just take the cut in profit in order not to pay him. Last summer about this time, all the crops on John's parents' property died but they had come back even more beautiful than before.

John could have really used the money. For the moment, anyway, it made his walk easier. During high school, he'd come back to these woods a lot and had never made it so quickly. The pond had been one of his other favorite spots but that had evaporated when he and Cassie closed the door on the Devils.

Or one of the doors.

John definitely wasn't comfortable thinking they'd never be back. He knew he was partially one of them but honestly thought if he just ignored it, it would go away. Maybe Cassie was right. Maybe he did need to try and act normal—get a job, eat people food— instead of being this creepy recluse.

On his walks, John always liked the quiet. And it wasn't really like it was quiet at all with the bird and insect and animal sounds. The breeze through the trees. It was quieter in the house but, in the house, his thoughts seemed too loud. Sometimes he would stop thinking for a few seconds and realize his jaws were clenched so tightly his ears were ringing. And Cassie lived in a "quiet" neighborhood but between the traffic, constant hum of the appliances, neighbors, and the occasional siren, it seemed like it was never quiet. Out here the only thing like that was the occasional airplane flying overhead. And he thought the natural sounds were good at creating just enough diversion to draw him out of his head.

He entered the woods, enjoying the relative gloom.

He became suddenly aware he was only feet from where his "initiation" had taken place. He didn't really know what else to call it. It wasn't like there was any exchange of knowledge or anything.

Their leader, the woman, had bitten him and then her legion of monsters had taken turns drinking his blood. That was a chilling thought. If they drank his blood like wine he wondered what effect it was having on Cassie.

But it was probably better not to think about that.

He remembered the large stone, now off to his right. Looking at it, he almost expected to see that eerie purplish light, smell the heady incense musk of their fire ... see the altar where he'd been restrained and initiated.

sacrificed

Yes, that may have been the intention. But before killing him they needed to use his body for something. They needed him to become one of them. But he hadn't done what they had wanted him to do. He and Cassie had kept that other world at bay.

And now they were still paying for it.

He just couldn't stop thinking about it.

Until he heard the screams.

He'd been so lost in his own head he thought they could have been going on for quite some time.

He took off running toward the screaming.

At one time, he was probably the most cowardly person he knew, although, at that time, he would have chalked it up to self-preservation. Since his biology had changed, he found himself quicker to anger. Unfortunately, the only person he usually had to get mad at was Cassie. But something in him seemed to rise up, welcome the confrontation. Maybe so he could lash out and shed blood and drink it up and finally become what Cassie called "the inevitable."

Nearly upon the house he became distracted by the man farther in the woods. The man was shouting "fuck" repeatedly. He looked homeless. He also looked like he was trying to destroy the woods.

John tried to pay half his attention to the crazy man and half his attention to the screaming.

Maybe the crazy man could help him.

"Hey!" John shouted.

The man turned to look at him, threw his arms up in the air, screamed like a girl, and took off running toward the Hixon place.

Aside from the offerings left on his doorstep, it was the strangest thing John had seen in a while.

It made him feel alive.

He thought the screams were coming from the direction of the abandoned house.

He crossed the yard and reached the porch quickly.

It was covered in mostly dried blood. Some of it was still sticky to the touch.

John realized he hadn't heard the screaming in a while.

He went into the house anyway.

Fourteen

After mercilessly butchering the whore in the hotel room, Ilya had fucked a pile of offal until her body came and went to sleep in the bloody, sticky bed. She woke up and took a shower. Put on the drab man's clothes, got back into his boring car, and continued onward toward Lynchville. If she wanted to revert back into her spirit form and leave Patrick Fishman as a quivering, weeping mess, she could have made it to Lynchville almost instantly. But, as with other human trappings, she had developed an enthusiasm for driving.

At the speeds she chose to travel, she thought it was probably the danger she liked more than the feeling of the road under the car.

It was mid-afternoon by the time she reached Lynchville.

If there was ever any doubt this was the place, her close proximity to it immediately erased that doubt.

The body she inhabited began trembling so much she had to pull the car off the road.

She put it into park and closed her eyes. Immediately she could *see* the town below her. She was first drawn to the pond she had first entered through but it now resembled a blank page. Empty. Not vibrating and alive as it had been the last time, ready to be changed with their energy. She was drawn to areas that had harbored human tragedy. That pond was a place where one of the owners, Herman Miller, had ritualistically drowned each newborn his wife had birthed. No one ever found out what he was doing and most of the infant bones had still been slowly decaying in the muck beneath the water.

Now her mind went to a new place.

This time it was a house.

She knew it as well as she knew any place in Lynchville.

Three different times the owners had been foreclosed upon. Three times the man of the house had killed his wife and whatever children had been there. And, even now, with no one living there, bad things were continuing to happen. She could see stains on the porch and knew it was blood. She heard screams and laughter.

Something else.

A deep, rumbling growl.

This place was powerful.

She thought she could do good work from there.

Feed the dark desires surging through her.

She took deep breaths with the host body, calmed herself. She wouldn't need this body for long.

She pulled back onto the state route and drove toward an old abandoned house on Suchling Road.

Fifteen

Cassie didn't know exactly what she was looking for and was planning on getting Melanie to help her but she wasn't at school. She didn't know if she was looking for a specific type of person or not. She thought it would probably be a girl or a group of girls.

Lynchville was a really small school so it wasn't like it had a lot of cliques.

It seemed like mostly jocks and cheerleaders so almost everyone else imitated the jocks and cheerleaders, making it pretty homogenous. There was a group of maybe five or six goth-type kids but she couldn't really figure out if they were into the Cure and death and vampires and stuff or if they just shopped at Hot Topic. That seemed too obvious, anyway.

It wasn't until she was sitting with her group of friends in the cafeteria at lunch that the obvious finally hit her.

It was probably one of *them*.

She didn't really talk a lot, period. And she hardly ever mentioned John. But still, they had to know.

And even thinking that, she thought the way they looked at her had changed. But that could be anything. It could be that she wasn't dating anyone from high school (not counting Melanie, which she was pretty sure no one would know about) or that she had a job that took up a lot of her free time or the fact that she was kind of involved in John's parents' disappearance.

"Something wrong?" Amber asked.

This startled Cassie. "Huh? Oh, no. Just tired."

"It sucks that you have to work."

"Well, I don't really *have* to."

"Oh, I thought you were partially supporting John."

The two guys at the table, Sean and Mike, started laughing. Cassie blushed. "I'm definitely not supporting him."

"Then maybe you're avoiding him."

"Of course not."

"Are you sure?"

"Why wouldn't I be? Why are you asking me this?"

"Because I think that Melanie might have a little something for him. She's been asking a lot of questions about him when you're not around."

"Like what kinds of questions? I've told her just about everything."

"I don't know. She was just asking if we'd ever met him, how long you two had been together. That kind of thing."

"Hm. Melanie's met him. She knows all that stuff."

"Well, maybe she just wanted our opinion on him then."

"And ...?"

"Honestly?"

"I'm pretty sure I know how you feel so go ahead."

"Creepy deadbeat."

Even though that was about what Cassie had expected and was, to a certain extent, how she felt herself, it still stung a little.

"I'm ... working on it." Cassie just didn't have the spirit to defend him today.

"Really?"

"Maybe. I still have a lot of thinking to do."

Amber reached out and grabbed her hand. "I really think you should. I think you'd be a lot happier."

Sixteen

Immediately after entering the house, John felt like he'd made a huge mistake. Part of him wanted to immediately turn around and leave. But then there was Cassie telling him he didn't do anything and he realized he couldn't. Besides, there was still the matter of the screaming.

He stood still and listened.

Maybe he still heard it. He couldn't be sure. It sounded faint, like it was coming from ever father away. Maybe it hadn't been coming from the hose at all. Still, while he was here, he should explore it. He wished he had something in the way of a weapon but there wasn't anything to grab. The house was completely, almost ecrily, empty.

"Hello?" he called, not really expecting to hear anything.

He didn't.

He wandered around the first floor. All the rooms were equally empty.

The house grew dimmer and he figured it was probably just a cloud passing over the sun.

His curiosity not yet slaked, he went upstairs. More of the same emptiness. Standing there, staring out at the dim woods through a missing window, he felt like the house was devoid of more than just objects. It felt devoid of a past, a history, anything. Or as though something were covering up those things.

Suddenly, deafening sound filled his head.

It started as laughter but became the same shrieking, piercing screaming he'd heard earlier.

The screams abruptly died away and he thought he heard a car.

He looked through the window and scanned the yard. A car came to a stop in the weedy driveway.

Shit. He needed to get out of here.

Pulse racing, he ran downstairs.

At the bottom he turned to run out the back door thinking whoever had arrived would probably come in the front. As soon as he turned into the kitchen to bolt for the door, he saw the man filling the doorway.

John had to come to a stop before he could turn around to go out the front door.

He looked into the man's black eyes. There was no white anywhere.

The man spoke.

He said, "Hello, John."

Seventeen

Cassie left the school and called Melanie before she'd left the parking lot. It was Friday and everyone was eager to be out. She waited for the line of cars, some of them filled with kids eagerly lighting cigarettes. Some of them were probably already cracking beers in anticipation of the weekend.

Melanie didn't answer.

Cassie left a message. "Hey. It's me. Missed you at school. I was just calling to make sure you were okay."

Maybe she really *was* sick. She knew Melanie's phone was usually within arm's reach and it wasn't like her not to answer it.

No need to panic, she thought.

Someone honked to let her in and she headed home to change for work.

Eighteen

John closed his eyes and shook his head.

There wasn't a man blocking the door.

It was a girl.

And it made a lot more sense for her to know his name than the imaginary man he hadn't recognized.

"Melanie?"

Did she blush? He thought maybe she blushed.

"Is that your car out there?"

"Yeah."

"What are you doing here?"

"What are *you* doing here?"

"I, um ... I asked you first."

Melanie smiled. "I came here to see you."

"Me? Why?"

"To see if you've received our offerings."

John didn't know what to say. He didn't know what to *think*.

"That was you?"

"I had some help."

Here it comes, John thought. Here comes the part where she had some help from the Devils and then, just like that, everything would be undone. He would be the same cowering person he was a year ago.

"Who?"

"Some friends from school."

"But why?"

"To help keep you alive."

He was stumped. He wasn't sure what he should do. He knew she was one of Cassie's friends. Possibly her closest friend and he had no idea what Cassie had told her. Cassie had told him she hadn't told anybody anything but if she *had*, and he tried to play dumb, it wasn't going to work very well. He decided to take that approach anyway.

"I'm not sure what you're talking about but I certainly don't drink blood to stay alive."

Melanie moved a few steps closer to him. Tiny, blond, blue-eyed, smiling sweetly even now, he couldn't imagine this girl draining the blood out of anything. Nor could he imagine her lying to him just to have fun with him.

"But I think you do," she said. "Cassie and I are pretty close. *Really* close. Before you get mad at her I want you to know that she didn't tell me that. She talks about you quite a bit, but she's careful to never mention what you really are. I've seen the cuts."

John thought about all the cuts he'd put on her body over the past several months. Maybe he should have just cut her in the same place over and over rather than cutting her in a different spot nearly every time.

"I notice you're not trying to defend yourself."

There wasn't anything for him to say.

"I love Cassie," Melanie said. Then she moved close to him and he felt a second of fear. Then he felt embarrassed by that. He doubted she was even five feet tall and probably not even a hundred pounds. "But I think I love you more."

She was practically touching him. He put his hands on her

shoulders and pushed her away slightly.

"Melanie ... You don't even know me."

"But I know what you are."

"That's crazy."

"And I know what Cassie says about you. I like that person. I want to be with that person. I want you to make me what you are."

"You need to stop and think about what you're saying."

"You need to listen to me. I can't force you. You can say no, but you need to hear what I have to say first."

John's head was a mess.

"Can we ... at least go outside?" he said. Maybe somewhere in the back of his head he was thinking he could take off running if he got too freaked out.

"After you," she said.

"You're not gonna stab me in the back are you?"

She let out a sound that was something like a giggle, but she didn't expressly say no. Maybe she's already stabbed enough people in the back, he thought.

He went out the front door, stepping into the tacky mess on the porch. Once they were outside in the fresh air, he felt a little better. It was definitely darker. Clouds completely covered the sky and he thought it could start raining soon. The weather in Ohio never ceased to fascinate him. He tested the railing on the porch and when he determined it wouldn't shatter with his weight, he leaned against it.

"Okay. I'm listening."

"Cassie's trying to leave you. It's been going on for a while. She's tired, John."

He knew things had been strained, but hearing it said like that was still shocking.

"How ...? What ...?"

"For me. She wants to leave you for me."

This wasn't helping a lot. He was glad he had the rail to lean against.

"Maybe ..." he stammered. "Maybe it's just all in your head."

"It's definitely not. She's told me."

"And you want to leave *her* for *me?*"

She moved close to him again. Now he felt trapped against the railing. The temperature had dropped. He could feel the warmth coming from her.

"I told you what I want."

John looked at Melanie. For so long, he'd really only thought about being with Cassie. Of course, that was helped by the fact that she was the only person he saw with any regularity who wasn't a 300 pound man.

Inevitable.

That word had been popping up a lot lately.

Both he and Cassie seemed to think so many things were inevitable.

John put his hands on Melanie's shoulders. This time it wasn't to push her away. He let them linger there. She was even smaller than Cassie. And yet not as bony. The difference did something to him.

He didn't do *anything.*

This felt like something.

He let his hands trail down her bare arms, his fingertips raising gooseflesh on her skin.

He moved his hands to her hips and pulled her into him. He was hard, almost painfully so, and his erection pressed against her stomach. She lifted her head up to him and he bent and kissed her. Her arms were then at the back of his head, her tongue entering his mouth. He knew if they didn't stop now, they probably wouldn't. He quickly unbuttoned her shirt, had his hands on her bra. It had been a long time since it was like this with Cassie. Usually she came over, took a shower, and just went to lie in bed naked, waiting for him to drink her blood and fuck her so she could feel as though her duties were fulfilled before getting the hell out.

"Take off your shirt," Melanie said.

Unhesitatingly, he did so. Cassie had probably been the only person to see him naked since he'd hit puberty.

Melanie moved her hands down his chest and stomach, opening the button on his pants. Then she turned around and pulled the hair off the back of her neck. He bent down, sucking on her ear, kissing her neck. She slowly ground herself against him. He undid the clasp on her bra, reached around and felt her small stiff nipples. He pinched them and she shuddered.

"I don't have anything," he said. "I mean, like, protection."

"Fuck it," she said. "Cassie's probably the only person either of us has slept with."

He wondered if that made her a virgin. He didn't think he cared. He unfastened her pants and slid them down over her striped underwear and round ass.

She turned back around, unzipped his pants and tugged them down with his underwear. She dropped to her knees in front of him. She ran her tongue around the head of his penis and he knew there wasn't any going back from this. She took him into her mouth and he was aware of the heat and the slight roughness of her tongue and gentle suction. He became aware of something else.

Here was fresh blood. Maybe that was half his arousal. This whole girl was like a gift, skin wrapped around pulsing, steaming blood.

He felt a fullness in his mouth.

This was the first time he'd actually felt himself change.

The last time, after he'd been infected, he was like a newborn. His consciousness blocked the change and he wandered his farm as a blind, hungry beast.

Now he could see and feel everything.

And he was very glad.

Melanie used a hand to rake the hair out of her eyes as she moved her head back and forth.

He grabbed her shoulders and pulled her up to her feet. She looked at him, noticed the change and, perhaps for the first time, realized how real this was, realized the Devils did exist and it was very far away from a romantic dream.

He moved behind her and pushed her against the railing, peeled down her underwear and entered her.

He thrust against her until she cried out, her fingernails scraping the railing. Then he leaned down and bit her on the shoulder. His teeth punctured the skin easily. He felt her sex contract against his spasming cock and he drank her blood greedily.

Nineteen

Ilya turned into the driveway to the house on Suchling Road. She stopped as soon as she saw a car already parked there. It must have recently pulled up because the driver was just now getting out. A girl. From this distance she looked really small.

This is going to be too easy, she thought.

She drove down the road until she found a chained access road. It was probably something used by the park rangers. She pulled just far enough onto the path to not be seen from the road. She didn't bother undoing the chain. She popped the trunk and got out of the car. She searched through the trunk until she found something close to what she was looking for. A bungee cord. It wasn't rope but it would do.

She had a number of reasons for returning to Lynchville and two of those would require her getting close to John and Cassie. She remembered them well. They were etched forever in her memory. Inhabiting a fat, boring, middle-aged man was no way to do that.

But, until he died, the body would make a nice meal.

She quickly fastened the bungee cord around her wrists and slid the cord far enough up the tree and down her arms to where she could no longer reach it to unfasten it. Exiting the body was simple for her. She'd done it so many times. It wasn't so easy on poor Patrick Fishman.

Now a vaporous mist hanging above him, she watched his eyes roll around in his head, heard his mouth jabbering, drool slicking his lips.

She made her way to the house.

And still couldn't believe her luck.

The girl standing in the door was not Cassie but Ilya could sense she *knew* Cassie.

And the guy standing in front of her ...

It was John.

Ilya didn't waste any time before swooping into Cassie's body and feeling the flood of emotions wash over her. Half of her story was already there. This girl *wanted* to become a Devil. All she would have to do would be to get John to infect her and then she would be more complete than she had been in a long time. Instead of immediately taking over the girl's brain, she let the girl continue on her own.

She was telling John things.

They made their way onto the front porch where the girl (Melanie) told John what she wanted. Ilya couldn't believe she'd gained this much knowledge in such a short period of time. She didn't even have to exert any control until John put his hands on her shoulder and the host wanted to back away.

But Ilya let John do what he wanted to do. It repulsed her. This guy's one crowning grain of self-esteem came from assuming he'd rid the world of her. She also knew what the result might be. For a Devil, the connection between sex and full transformation was very strong.

She didn't think she'd felt anything as sweet as when he plunged his rediscovered fangs into her shoulder.

Now she had him.

It might take him a while to notice, if he ever did, but she had him.

Twenty

The first thing he thought when he tasted her blood was that there was something wrong. He dismissed the thought and kept drinking, though. He was so hungry. Maybe something just seemed off because he'd drunk nothing but Cassie's for so long and never in this quantity.

By the time he pulled away from her, he felt disgusted with himself. His penis dangled flaccid between his thighs, slick with his and Melanie's juices. The blood sat in his stomach like milk that had gone sour.

And Melanie now acted like this wasn't something she wanted at all. She avoided looking at him, bending to pull up her underwear he hadn't even bothered removing all the way. Plucking the rest of her clothes up from the porch and putting them on. He felt like she would have left right away but there was a boom of thunder and it started pouring.

He pulled up his pants and fought the urge to vomit off the side of the porch.

"I'm not feeling well," he said.

She didn't say anything.

He didn't know why, but he went back into the house. It wasn't like there was anything in there to comfort him. It just seemed like the thing to do.

In the house, the room began spinning around him. He felt kind of scared. He'd never felt anything like this before. Maybe it was the start of the flu or maybe he was just overwhelmed with guilt. He sat down on the floor, leaning back against the wall.

He thought it was kind of odd that Melanie never came in to see how he was doing.

Right now he felt sick but he didn't know how to feel about the whole Melanie thing. Had she really slept with Cassie? John didn't even know Cassie was or ever had been into girls.

This was too much.

He'd have to think about it later.

Twenty-one

Cassie had just put on her work clothes and was ready to head back out to the car when she got a text from Melanie.

"You around?"

Cassie texted her back and said she was on her way to work. "Pick you up around 11?" she added.

"Sure."

Cassie couldn't help smiling.

Twenty-two

Ilya turned the display on her phone off and thought, "Easier and easier." Now she just had to kill a few hours of time. There was a guy in the woods who needed tending to, she thought.

Twenty-three

Wayne stood at the edge of the woods holding his shriveling dick in his hand and wondering what the hell had just happened. He watched the guy go back into the house and the girl get back in the car and drive away.

Wayne had fled when he'd first seen the guy in the woods but it was shortly after sprinting away that he'd regretted it. He should have asked the guy what the hell he was doing on his property, even though he wasn't sure this was his property or not, advanced on him, and beaten him to a pulp. But by the time he'd returned to his senses, stopped abusing the woods, and doubled back around, the guy was gone.

Wayne thought it was even possible that was the guy who'd been making the woman make all those horrible screams.

But that theory was mostly debunked when the girl in the car pulled up and went around to the back of the house.

Now Wayne realized his current vantage point wasn't the best. He could only see the front door. He circled around the perimeter of the woods, trying his best to stay out of sight until he would be able to see if anyone left from either the front or the back doors.

Unless he'd already left, the guy was still in there.

The girl and the boy had then come out the front door. Wayne had some voyeuristic tendencies and, okay, so he hadn't slept with a woman since Alison had kicked him out. He was a little hard up. The Internet provided as much porn as he could tolerate but there was something about seeing a real girl in the flesh that he didn't have the money to buy. Not that he thought what happened would actually happen. But perhaps that was just the mindset of someone who had been practically raised on porn. Sex could break out at any given time under any given circumstances. That was one of the reasons he always kept a condom in his wallet. It was true that never in his thirty-plus years had sex actually happened that way to him or that he'd observed sex happening in that way but, well, maybe it was the one grain of optimism he still had left.

So when the guy started unbuttoning the girl's shirt, he was immediately hard.

Being that he was in the woods and the only other people around were preoccupied, he undid his pants and pulled his penis out.

The couple started going at it and Wayne came faster than he had in a long time.

And then the guy had changed.

Even from this distance, Wayne thought it looked like he grew slightly taller and more sinewy. His mouth filled with teeth. Wayne almost cried out when the guy lowered his head and bit the girl. He tried to tell himself he would have stopped it if the girl didn't seem to be enjoying it so much. Then, just like that, it was all over. The guy staggered around and went back into the house. The girl put on her clothes and left.

This was all too much.

Wayne sat down on the ground and leaned back against the tree. He checked his phone for the time and messages he didn't have. He thought about calling Major but knew that would just make him sadder than he already was.

He'd give it a few minutes and, if the guy never left, then Wayne would assume he already had. Then he would go take a scan around the house to make sure the guy wasn't in there.

No he wouldn't.

Who was he kidding?

He'd just seen that guy turn into a monster.

Wayne had grown up in Lynchville where rumors of the Devils abounded. He'd written a book about vampires and referred to them as Devils.

Until a few minutes ago he'd never believed in them.

Now he did.

He wished he'd turned his camera phone on. He had it in his hand now. He was ready. He knew it was pointless. No one would think a vampire video coming from him would be anything but a hoax.

But he wasn't going to sit here and fool himself into thinking he would do something he wasn't.

He didn't mind the occasional thrill but if, you know, actual *death* were involved, he tended to avoid it. That's why he never went into the military.

And despite writing about vampires, he couldn't see why people romanticized them like they did. To an extent, he supposed being a vampire would cure a lot of humanity's fears. Being a vampire, one would have power and eternal life. No one wanted to die and no one liked being at the bottom of the food chain.

However, he assumed most people were still basically moral creatures. For one thing, vampirism was a slap in the face to God and Christianity. Here were, essentially, humans with godlike powers. Humans who had to sacrifice other humans to stay alive. Which was another moral issue. If humans were made to kill other humans that easily, he didn't think a police force, no matter what its size, could provide adequate protection.

Wayne continued to watch until he dozed off.

It was the longest he'd slept in a while.

Twenty-four

Cassie closed down her register and left work as quickly as she could. She wanted to get to John's, let him drink from her, avoid any major arguments, and get to Melanie's as quickly as possible. She needed to see if she could enlist her help in finding out who was leaving the offerings. Of course, after talking to Amber and a few of her other friends throughout the day, Cassie thought she had a pretty good idea of who it was. In which case, it was probably a lot more stupid and harmless than she had originally thought. And if Melanie was going to confess, Cassie thought a nice warm period of post-coital bliss would be the perfect time for her to do that.

She reached John's house in record time. She wondered if she could get him to drink a couple days' worth so she wouldn't have to fool with coming tomorrow. Of course, he would want to know why she wasn't coming and that would probably start an argument, which was on her agenda to actively avoid.

She pulled up into his driveway, not even bothering to take the keys out of the ignition. She gave the door her customary two knock warning before opening it and going in.

The house was quiet, but it always was.

"Hello?" she said.

Usually he called out from somewhere in the house, but this time she didn't hear anything. Maybe he was in the shower. She didn't know how he could stand to take cold showers, even in the summer.

She walked upstairs to the only bathroom with a shower in it. The door was wide-open. It was, of course, dark, but no darker than the rest of the house.

She went into the bedroom to make sure he wasn't asleep. He usually just slept on the couch, but she wanted to make sure. She went through the rest of the rooms to make sure he wasn't there. Nothing turned up.

This was the first time he hadn't been there.

She didn't know if she should try to find him, stick around to see if he came home, or just leave. This latter option wouldn't have even entered her mind if they hadn't been arguing so much lately. She knew John was not a confrontational person. This was exactly the way he would do things. Just avoid her long enough for her to worry about him and then come back after she'd spent a night wondering if he were dead or alive, what it would be like to really lose him. Of course, he wouldn't be able to keep it up for more than a day or two or he really would die. He needed her way more than she needed him.

She went out on the front porch and yelled his name, waited for any type of response but all she heard were the insects and the peepers.

She texted Melanie. "U home?"

Cassie could leave tonight and not feel too badly about it. If there still wasn't a sign of him tomorrow, she would put more effort into looking for him.

What if the person who'd left the offerings had found him?

What if it really was Melanie?

Her phone vibrated in her hand and she almost dropped it.

It was just a message from Melanie that said, "Yes."

"Okay," Cassie announced to the darkness. "If you really are here and are just being an asshole, I'm leaving. If you're here tomorrow, I think we're going to have to talk. If you're not here because you're *still* being an asshole, then I'm done. I hope you understand that. I didn't have this much time to waste."

If nothing else, saying those things made her feel a little better.

She texted Melanie back: "Be right there."

She still felt slightly guilty when she left.

Twenty-five

When Ilya got in the car, she knew instinctively where her home was. Many of her kind shunned modern amenities but she thought that was probably just because they were overwhelmed. The only reason to be overwhelmed was because things were so different than they had been. There was certainly nothing difficult about new things. They were so easy to operate it seemed like everything was designed for a six-year-old. She thought a child could probably drive with relative ease if their legs were long enough to reach the pedals.

Driving back to her house, Ilya had gleaned from host Melanie that she was in school and hadn't gone today because she was panicked about something at that house. She had been as shocked as John to run into him there.

Ilya wanted to go back to the host's house and spend some time with her memories and feelings before they died away completely. Not surprisingly, as with almost everything else in Lynchville, this girl seemed rich and complex. Unlike that Patrick guy.

When Ilya left the house, she'd gone back to where she left Patrick's car. Having had John feast on her had made her hungry as well. She had ventured into the woods to feast on Patrick. As Patrick, back in the hotel room with the whore, whatever morality he'd had had been overridden by his surprisingly fierce and intact sexual drive. But if she had eliminated that, it would have been very difficult to get him to do the things he'd done—especially that early in the transformation.

But she was able to use this girl to eviscerate and feast upon Patrick with relative ease.

Ilya almost thought it was like she'd done it before.

Or maybe she just knew all about survival.

Regardless, Ilya thought there was a lot to know about Melanie.

When she got to Melanie's house, she unlocked the door and went quickly and quietly to the bathroom. She washed the blood off, wrapped a towel around herself, and went to lie down in Melanie's bed.

In her spirit form, Ilya was able to focus on breathing, expanding above her physical locale and taking it in, even focusing on specific parts of it. Of course it wasn't really breathing, vapor didn't breathe, but that was the closest anthropomorphization she could think of.

Inside the girl's body, she was able to do much the same thing. She closed her eyes and breathed deeply and evenly. Let herself expand into Melanie's brain and viscera. Ilya had found there were almost as many memories in the muscle as there were in the brain.

She didn't know if she got the complete story, but the pieces she did get were scary enough. Well, scary to a normal person. Ilya found them exhilarating. It was always refreshing to see the power of the Devils at work on the young, especially when people like her didn't even have to do anything to provoke it. Unless turning John would have been considered provoking it.

It seemed her obsession had bloomed from talking with Cassie and her friends. Cassie didn't think any of them knew anything, but they'd pretty much heard the entire story. While Cassie and John had been the only people on that farm the last time Ilya had opened the door, Lynchville was a receptor, meaning everyone was connected to that other world in more ways than they could imagine. Many of the specifics came to them in dreams. Many of them simply arose in stories and rumors. It was a small town. People talked. And since it was a pretty boring town, when they spoke they had a tendency to elaborate if for nothing more than to make things more interesting.

There was also a part of Melanie that resented Cassie. Why did the interesting things always happen to her? Melanie had been with Stasia and Mark and Anthony and they had all been drinking and one of the guys decided they should do something as a kind of joke. Maybe they got the idea from *Carrie*. Although, at the beginning anyway, it was a more watered down version. They'd found a pig farm and caught the smallest pig they could, drained the blood into a metal bucket, and left it in front of John's door.

That first time, one of the guys had knocked on the door before running back into the woods to join the rest of them. John had opened the door. From what Cassie had said, he probably didn't sleep at night. He'd looked down at the bucket of blood and the note. He'd quickly looked up and scanned the surroundings and Melanie had had a panicked thought that he could see them but didn't really care because she figured he was mostly harmless anyway.

The next week she had the urge to do it again. Stasia agreed and Mark agreed because he and Stasia were sleeping together and he agreed to everything she requested because he was afraid if he didn't then she would stop sleeping with him. Anthony said he was out. He'd probably only done it originally to score points with Melanie since it seemed like Cassie was already taken.

Melanie was fairly persuasive. Maybe manipulative was the right word. She wasn't the prettiest or most popular girl at school but people seemed drawn to her. Her parents were loaded and left town a lot so she had a lot of parties at her house. Her dad must have been friends with Chief Bowsman or something because her parties never seemed to get broken up. There were always a lot of people from the high school there. Sometimes, there were even people from Wright State and UD. Very occasionally, there were people there from Dunham. Sometimes Melanie didn't even know half the people there. Maybe it was just the power of social networking.

Therefore, to be on Melanie's bad side was to effectively eliminate yourself from having a high school social life.

So when Melanie had told Stasia and Mark that, this time, she wanted to use *human* blood, they had initially refused but still listened to her argument.

And maybe it was more than just her good social standing or her powers of persuasion. The Devils' power was all-pervasive in Lynchville. It had a way of touching people as though it rose from the very soil. Ilya supposed, in a way, it did. The powerful ones had mostly gone away or moved to places where the hunting was easier. There were very few as powerful as she was. But there were hundreds of them, mostly in spirit form, who could move into people, simply for amusement or, sometimes, to influence them. When the door to that other place was closed, as it was now, their powers weren't as strong. But they were still there. That could have gone a long way toward explaining the familiarity Ilya felt when entering Melanie's body.

Melanie explained to the two others that they wouldn't have to kill anyone. She would do the killing. She just wanted them there. Mark had said something about accomplices and she said there wasn't any way they'd be caught so there wasn't anything to worry about. She worked their morality by telling them she would go into bars and pick up guys so whoever she ended up killing would basically be a pedophile.

Mark tried to argue with this. He told her that sixteen was hardly a child and said he and Stasia had had sex and wondered if that made them both pedophiles.

Melanie had said it didn't because they were both underage and it was still wrong for an adult to do that with a teenager. She didn't believe that at all, but she would make any argument to strengthen the case. She knew she already had them, anyway.

So the first victim had been a kitchen helper at Chef Uncle's. She had waited for him outside the Nilbog Roadhouse and hooked him before he went in.

Sometimes, she had thought, it took doing something you were never expected to do to unlock something inside of you.

Stasia and Mark had gone wild that first time. Technically, Melanie had been the one doing the killing but both Mark and Stasia went above and beyond in the "clean-up".

They were progressively into it over the next two killings, eventually culminating in the loser they had killed a couple of nights ago. She had been seeing Cassie for about the past month and telling herself it wasn't because of the girl's close proximity to John. Melanie saw how much Stasia and Mark enjoyed this and she had been working up the courage to ask Cassie to join her. She really thought she would say yes but she needed to get past the feeling that Cassie would think she was using her. Which really wasn't true. She did love Cassie. She just wanted to be what John was. She wasn't really too concerned with pursuing John because, try as she had, she just wasn't really into guys. Another part of her had just contemplated waiting. Melanie thought, eventually, John would turn Cassie and then Cassie could turn her and they wouldn't really have much of a need for John.

Melanie had told her mom she felt sick that morning because she had had an odd feeling about that house. More and more, Melanie had learned to trust those feelings. As she got closer to it, she started to think maybe it was just the usual post-murder panic. It was usually dark when they did their clean-up and she was sure they missed things but the house was so in the middle of nowhere that it usually didn't bother her. So, anyway, she figured she could go clean up a little, sure the porch could use it, at least, and just check to make sure things were generally okay.

And she had seen John there.

And then the two of them were not alone.

Ilya opened her eyes, feeling informed and somewhat rested. Now the only thing she had to decide was whether to stay in this body or try to enter Cassie.

But she didn't think she would do that.

She wanted to watch the bitch suffer from the outside.

Twenty-six

It was dark by the time Wayne awoke. He felt good. Maybe he'd had a good dream but he didn't remember the specifics of it. There was a moment of confusion before the specifics came back to him.

He checked his phone to make sure it still had power.

It did. That was good.

He'd decided he was going to look for the Devil in the house. He didn't know why. He didn't know if anything would come of it. Mainly he just wanted to see if he was still in there. Maybe that was his base. Maybe he lived there.

Or it was possible the transformation he'd seen was just a mild hallucination and he was looking for someone to pick a fight with.

Or just simple curiosity.

He had one vampire book languishing somewhere other than the bookshelves of America and it was probably time for him to write another one. Before writing his other books, he'd gone through a similar pattern. Happiness that he'd finished a book. Intense depression once he started sending it out and the rejections started to come back. In the case of *Vampires in Devil Town* that was followed by another period of happiness once the book had been accepted and continuing through the whole publication process. Followed by intense depression at mostly nonexistent sales. During those periods of mania and depression, he tended not to write much of anything. Maybe the occasional short story if he could complete a first draft in a night or two.

There usually then had to be some vaguely to flagrant life changing event that threw him into gear.

Meeting Alison had been one. Getting his bachelor's had been another. The birth of Major, of course. Moving into a house where he thought they would be spending much of the rest of their lives had been the latest.

Now he would have thought that divorce, returning home, and finding both of his parents had died in a house fire would have been enough.

But, apparently not. As with most other things, he found himself wanting more and more.

He ascended the creaky steps to the porch. The door wasn't even shut all the way. He opened the flashlight app on his phone and shined it into the darkness of the house.

He didn't have to go far before he nearly stumbled over the Devil. He didn't look so much like a Devil now. Just a boy. Well, maybe not really a boy. A young man. No older than early twenties though. As Wayne had grown older, he'd become a terrible judge of age.

He shined the flashlight on the kid's face.

No response.

His chest rose and fell with his breathing so Wayne knew he had to be alive. He guessed he was okay but felt like he should make sure, more out of curiosity than any kind of goodwill. He nudged the guy's leg with his foot.

"Hey," he said, not too loudly. He didn't want to startle him. Wayne knew *he* hated to be woken up from naps.

The nudge didn't elicit so much as a change in his breathing.

Maybe that girl had drugged him or something. Or maybe the

Devil got really tired after fucking and biting an attractive-at-least-from-a-distance girl.

The proper thing to do would have been to call the police and tell them he'd seen a suspicious person entering an abandoned home so he didn't sound like a raving maniac but Wayne didn't want anything to do with Chief Bowsman and his goons ever again.

He reached down to grab the guy's shoulder and really shake it proper but his hand passed through it and he found himself using his hand to prop himself on the wall so he didn't fall over.

He straightened up and looked down at the guy.

Only there was no guy.

What the hell was going on?

"Fuck me," Wayne said to no one. Then he paused to think about it, wondered if that girl was still around somewhere and said, "No, seriously, fuck me. Please."

That would have been too good to be true.

He looked down where the guy was only a moment before. His phone had fallen asleep so he turned it back on, the bright glow of the flashlight app beaming out.

There definitely wasn't anything there.

Now he guessed the only question was if he had *ever* been there.

Wayne seriously doubted that was the case. He wasn't the type of guy to see things or have hallucinations. If he were, he would have experienced one by now. Few people wanted to believe in things like ghosts and monsters more than him but, up until a short while ago, he hadn't had any inclination to believe those things existed. Plus he was a masochist, so he'd naturally lean toward the belief that made his life the most difficult. In this case, that was the belief that there was something seriously fucked up going on here.

The easiest thing to do would have been to get back in his car and drive out to the interstate until he found a cheap hotel, buy a twelve pack from a gas station, take a long shower, drink until he felt like throwing up or, hell, going all the way and drinking until he couldn't physically drink any more, passing out in a bed that was probably crawling with things but had mostly clean sheets, getting into the car the next morning and driving back to Illinois. Maybe not necessarily back to Alison but ... close.

He wiped a hand over his face. He felt crusty. He wiped his hand over it again.

He wasn't going to do the easy thing at all.

If anything, he was going to do the most difficult thing imaginable.

He was going to believe it all.

He thought about this on his walk back to maybe his/maybe his aunt's burned out house.

He rationalized it thusly:

He'd grown up hearing all the rumors and legends about the Devils in Lynchville. All rumors, no matter how preposterous, had at least a grain of truth to them. Wayne, basically an atheist since his best friend had died of brain cancer in the third grade, had chosen not to believe any of them. Even while writing *Vampires in Devil Town* the connection was lost on him. He thought he could write something like that because it was something he was interested in but not necessarily invested in. He could have probably written about Jesus just as easily if the texts surrounding him weren't so incredibly dry. So, maybe, if he chose to believe in everything, he would see Lynchville with new eyes. It was like the first time he'd drunk coffee made the way it was supposed to be made or drank a microbrew beer. He'd found both of them almost pungently strong. But after finding out that was the way they were supposed to taste, he had a greater appreciation for them. And then it was hard to go back to the weak stuff.

Maybe he was just trying to appreciate Lynchville.

Once back at the house, he checked his email.

There was one with the subject: "Money From Africa!!!"

He almost deleted it until he saw that the sender was Gregory Seymour, his publisher. The only reason Wayne could see for Seymour giving it that subject was because Seymour was an ass.

He'd probably open it to find a deposit with the almost sarcastic total of five dollars or something.

But he did a double take at the bank notification in the body of the email.

It was nearly 1500 dollars.

Not a staggering sum but, at its previous rate, that was more than Wayne stood to make off *Vampires* in three years.

Either something really good was happening to it or Seymour was laundering money somehow.

Wayne didn't care either way.

He was looking at the town with new eyes.

1500 dollars was enough money for a really good bender.

What better place to start exploring the town than Chef Uncle's?

Then he remembered the vomit.

Maybe he should try Bunk's or Nilbog's instead.

He decided to go to Nilbog's because it sounded weird and, from what he remembered about his high school days, Bunk's was more of a biker bar.

He checked his wallet to make sure he hadn't thrown his debit card out in a fit of rage. Once he confirmed its rightful place, he hopped in the car and headed toward town.

Twenty-seven

Cassie sent Melanie a message letting her know she was there. It was Friday night, she'd swiped a bottle of wine from the store and she planned on taking Melanie back to her house, plying her with aforementioned wine, and then grilling her about John. But, after Melanie slid into the passenger seat all freshly showered, gave her a beaming smile and a kiss, and said, "Hi, I've been waiting all day to see you," she kind of forgot about the trial she had planned. Now she just wanted to take her back to her bedroom and fuck her until both of their tongues were raw and their legs shaky.

Cassie's parents usually went out on Fridays and sometimes didn't come back until two or three. That was if both of them weren't too drunk to drive and they decided to get a hotel wherever they were "going out". Obviously, there weren't a lot of places in Lynchville for them to go so they usually ended up going to Dayton or Cincinnati.

That was good. Cassie thought she might want to cause Melanie make some noise.

When they pulled up into her driveway, Cassie turned to Melanie and said, "So, are you in the mood?"

She laughed softly and said, "Like you wouldn't believe."

Cassie grabbed her giant purse with the bottle of wine in it and, once outside the car, grabbed Melanie's hand, started to lead her up to the bedroom and then changed her mind. They'd never done this anywhere except her bedroom. A change of scenery seemed exciting. She led Melanie through the house and out the sliding glass back door until they stood on the porch. While getting caught was a small part of the thrill, Cassie thought if her parents did come home while they were in the act, and they left the porch lights off, they probably wouldn't even know she and Melanie were out there.

"Out here?" Melanie said.

Cassie said nothing. Just laughed.

Cassie was still in her work uniform, unshowered, and felt kind of like a pig. Still, something about this kind of made her hot. She probably wouldn't let Melanie go down on her, but there were plenty of other things they could do.

Cassie put her small hands around Melanie's thin neck and pulled her close. They kissed slowly, their tongues playing in each other's mouths. Cassie thought this was one of the reasons she preferred having sex with Melanie than John or some other guy. There wasn't any big rush. And, since Melanie had the same parts as her, she knew how to make her feel really good. With Melanie, there wasn't a big erection waving in front of her like a balloon that it was her job to pop. It was just a slow, almost maddening boil of sensation. Sometimes a number of climaxes. Sometimes just a steady build to one huge climax. And sometimes numbness and fatigue set in before the big climax was reached but, as the old saying went, sometimes the journey was the best part.

Melanie wore a skin tight t-shirt with no bra and equally tight skinny jeans. Cassie lifted up the hem of her t-shirt and rubbed the small of her back and the almost invisible down that grew there, let a couple of fingers sneak into the waistband of her pants, between the tops of her ass cheeks. Melanie sucked on the side of Cassie's neck.

"You smell ... like a grocery store." She laughed.

Cassie liked the way Melanie's mouth and tongue felt too much to laugh or say anything.

Cassie backed away from her and stood there. Since the porch light was off and they hadn't bothered to turn the kitchen light on, the only thing illuminating them was the dim light of the moon.

Melanie stood there, looking kind of clueless, like she didn't know what to do without Cassie in her arms. Cassie liked it. It made her look vulnerable or something.

"I don't know what's different," Cassie said, "but you look really really good today."

"Maybe you just want me more than usual."

"Maybe. Maybe. I want you to stand right there and watch me take off my clothes."

"Your gross grocery store clothes?"

"Exactly." She liked how quickly Melanie picked up on things.

Cassie kicked off her canvas shoes, peeled off her socks and balled them up in the shoes. She pulled off her shirt and let it drop. Slowly unbuttoned and unzipped her khaki pants, letting them fall to the ground and stepping out of them. She unfastened her bra and let it drop. Her breasts, though small, felt heavy, the nipples like little dark knots.

"Your breasts are so small," Melanie said.

"I'm sorry."

"Keep going."

Cassie covered her chest with her left arm and slowly pulled down her plain white underwear with her right hand.

Melanie looked between Cassie's legs. "When was the last time you shaved? It's a little stubbly."

"I know. I'm sorry. It's been a week at least."

"My tongue'll bleed if I lick that thing."

"I know. I don't expect you to."

"I don't think I will."

Now Cassie covered her sex with her right hand.

"Now you," Cassie said.

Melanie shook her head. "You lost control the first time you apologized. I want you to lean over the table."

Cassie turned to the round glass patio table and leaned over it. It was damp and covered in dew so she rested on her elbows.

Melanie stood by her side and said, "No," before pulling her arms straight out in front of her until her chest lay flat on the cool wet glass.

Melanie did something behind her. Cassie turned her head to look at her and Melanie said, "No. You stare straight ahead."

Cassie turned her head to stare out into the dark.

Melanie now stood on the other side of the table in front of Cassie. She had the bottle of wine in one hand and one of Cassie's shoes in the other. She forced Cassie's head down on the table until she rested on her left cheek, her earring making a click against the glass.

"Open your mouth," Melanie said.

Cassie did.

"Wider."

Cassie opened her mouth as wide as it would go.

Melanie slid the bottle in.

"I want you to suck on this. I want you to pretend it's a dick. Can you do that?"

"Mm-hm," Cassie mumbled around the bottle.

"I thought you might be able to. I got this idea when you suggested we both fuck around with John."

Melanie pushed the bottle in a little farther.

"You're not sucking. This is a big dick, remember. Maybe it's John's dick only, if you accidentally bite down on it, it's probably going to hurt an awful lot."

Melanie stood behind Cassie.

She brought the shoe down harshly on Cassie's ass. Cassie's first instinct was to clench her teeth but she couldn't with the bottle there.

"That was for trying to look and see what I was doing. Keep that bottle in your mouth. You can use your hands if you have to. Now, how many hours did you work today?"

Cassie tried to mumble, "Six."

Melanie brought the shoe down again. "I couldn't hear you. Show me with your fingers."

Cassie held up both hands with three fingers on each raised.

"Six?"

"Mm-hm."

"That's six hours you could have spent with me. That means I'm going to hit you six times with this shoe. As hard as I can. Now I want you to put the bottle as deep in your mouth as you can and take your hands away. If you still have the bottle in your mouth when I'm finished, then you'll get a reward."

Cassie slid the bottle into her mouth until her teeth touched it and she was close to gagging.

Without any warning, Melanie brought the shoe down on her ass again. It hurt pretty badly but it also made her tingle between the legs and she found herself anticipating the next one. By the third hit, the pleasure was mostly gone and now it just stung. The bottle came close to falling out of her mouth until she fought the urge to push it back in and instead used suction. The bottle was heavy and it was hard to do but it took her mind off the remainder of the swats.

Melanie pressed her hips against Cassie's ass and leaned over her to make sure the bottle was still in place.

"Very good," she whispered into her ear before sliding the bottle from Cassie's mouth.

Her jaws felt numb.

"Don't turn around," Melanie said.

Cassie continued staring out at the dark woods surrounding her backyard. She closed her eyes, imagined Melanie behind her. She felt her drag the spit wet tip of the bottle down her spine and between her buttocks. Then she felt it rub against the lips of her sex, the slightly rough surface of the cork contrasting with the slickness of the glass. Melanie began to press it in. She was no stranger to having things put in her but John was not exceptionally huge and she wasn't sure how much of it she could take. Melanie continued sliding it in until Cassie gasped because it felt like she was ripping open. Then she pushed it in just a little more. Cassie fought the urge to slam her palm down on the table. She clenched her teeth and hissed an intake of breath.

She felt Melanie's free hand on the small of her back. Now she was kissing Cassie's still stinging ass cheeks. Melanie's tongue went to the crack of her ass and slowly slid down until it pressed her anus. This was something she hadn't felt before. Her lower stomach immediately went into a spasming knot. Melanie slid the bottle out a little and then pushed it back in again. Almost simultaneously, she forced her tongue into Cassie's anus. Cassie let out a moan and fought the urge to cry louder.

Melanie continued moving the bottle in and out of Cassie's vagina. She pulled her tongue out of her ass just long enough to bite her buttock playfully. It was like a more concentrated sting than the shoe. She liked it.

Melanie returned her tongue to Cassie's anus and worked it in as far as she could. Cassie bit her tongue and clutched the edge of the table with her hands, all of her muscles drawn tight. She didn't know how many times she came. It was like with the bottle so far in her, the muscles couldn't contract to give her the one big orgasm so it was all of these little tremors.

Before she could protest, Melanie pulled the bottle out of her and pressed it against her asshole.

She was going to tell her to stop but she put her mouth where the bottle had been and began alternately sucking at her juices and flicking her clitoris with her tongue, all the while working the bottle in as far as it would go, which wasn't that much.

After a few minutes of this, Cassie didn't think she could stand up anymore. All of her muscles felt like rubber.

Melanie again leaned over her back to speak into her ear. Cassie could smell herself on her. "Maybe we should go to your room now?"

"M'kay." Cassie felt a little embarrassed. She didn't think she'd ever lost that much control with John or Melanie before.

While Cassie gathered her clothes, Melanie went into the kitchen, washed the bottle off in the sink, grabbed some glasses and the corkscrew.

Cassie stepped into the kitchen. She could feel herself running down the inside of her thigh. "We should go ahead and open that down here. They'll notice if it's gone."

"They won't notice you upstairs eating me out but they'll notice a missing corkscrew?"

"They like their wine and respect their daughter's privacy."

"Unless she's getting fucked by a guy."

"Well, we were sort of on the living room couch."

"What a whore."

Cassie laughed. "I think I just demonstrated that."

"Perfectly. Let's go get drunk."

They went upstairs and proceeded to do just that. Her parents came home sometime during that but they didn't even bother knocking on Cassie's door to tell her they were there because the only light she had on was a night light. Her phone vibrated and she figured it was probably just one of them texting her that they were home.

Cassie hadn't bothered putting on any clothes. She'd just wrapped herself in a sheet and played her sex mix playlist on her computer. It was mostly James Blake, SBTRKT, and a lot of other slow electronic music.

They lay in bed and drank the wine. Cassie felt too good to bring up anything too heavy. By the time they were nearly finished with the bottle of wine it was well after midnight and they were both exhausted.

But Melanie was still wearing all those clothes.

Cassie slowly peeled off her t-shirt and jeans, something she had wanted to do ever since seeing her step out of her house. She left her black underwear on. She crawled down between Melanie's legs.

Melanie rubbed the top of her head and said, "You don't have to."

"Want." Cassie raised her head up to look at Melanie. "I *want* to."

"I'm pretty drunk," Melanie slurred. "I'm not going to stop you. It'll feel good."

Cassie bit at her through the underwear, making sure to breathe heavily and warmly on her. When Melanie's underwear were thoroughly soaked, Cassie pulled them down to her knees. Melanie was definitely not stubbly. It looked like she had shaved earlier that day. Cassie loved this. She licked and sucked all around it before plunging her tongue into Melanie. There was a lot of girl come and Cassie thought she caught a slight hint of something fruity. Maybe Melanie had taken the day off school for vaginal maintenance.

Melanie was good at coming without moaning. She writhed around on the bed while Cassie tended to her. She shuddered violently and Cassie drank everything she could from inside her and slid up on the bed next to her. Melanie rolled over and pressed her ass against Cassie's hips. Cassie kissed the back of her head and put her arms around her.

Before she closed her eyes for the night, she noticed the bite mark on her shoulder.

She thought about telling her to get out and then thought that might be a blown opportunity.

Now she wouldn't have to have the dreaded conversation at all.

She could just follow her.

Cassie didn't know how she could have been so stupid.

It all made sense.

Melanie just wanted to be close to her because she was close to John.

It all made *perfect* sense. Melanie had not come to school today so she could be with John. John hadn't been there today because he was feeling guilty, not because he was mad at her.

She didn't know if what happened between her and Melanie tonight had been overcompensation or sadism.

She wanted to think some more but not with Melanie lying beside her. Besides, she was exhausted and the alcohol made it twice as hard to think. Impossible to think logically.

Twenty-eight

Nilbog's didn't go very well. Wayne pounded three shots of whiskey as soon as he got there. He tried to talk about the Devils as though they were a sports team.

"How bout those Devils?" was his opening line.

There were maybe only fifteen to twenty people in Nilbog's and, after questioning/shouting at the first ten, the rest avoided him when they saw him coming. One really rude guy who was many teeth shy of a mouthful told Wayne he would punch him if he came closer.

While the patrons Wayne was able to talk to were not very forthcoming with their own stories, a few of them didn't mind him telling his story, which was what he'd seen earlier. Typically concluded with, "You believe that shit?"

From most of the reactions, he couldn't tell if they believed it or not. He was hoping it would be like an incest survivors' meeting or something where one person tells his story and everyone else has a story to share. It wasn't like that at all. Tired of the passive resistance, Wayne found a table in a darkened corner of the bar and blacked/passed out.

He was roused by the burly female bartender telling him he

couldn't sleep in here and was he walking or would he like her to call him a cab? Wayne tried to slur the word, "Driving," and she'd mentioned having to call the police. So then he slurred the word "walking" and that seemed to ward her off. She was replaced by a couple of larger men who were eager to help him out the door. Stupid fuckers, Wayne thought. People would do anything if they thought a free drink was involved.

Wayne wasn't exactly sure, but he thought maybe he said, "I'm so lonely! I'm just trying to make friends!" on his way out. Then he did specifically recall going around to the side of the building into the dark alleyway, bracing himself against the wall, and vomiting. He remembered this because that was when he saw *her*.

The words "teenage dream" flashed across his eyes. He held out his hand and asked if she wanted to take him to Taco Bell, he was buying. She smirked and said she had a better idea in mind. He asked if her parents were home and she gently but firmly asked him to be quiet.

She took his hand and walked him to his car. He started to open the driver's side door. She shook her head and held out her hand.

"What? I'm fine," he protested.

She gestured out of the parking lot to the street. A darkened police cruiser sat there and Wayne could imagine Chief Bowsman sitting behind the wheel, fisting donuts into his mouth and chugging coffee. So he handed the keys to the girl. And then it dawned on him this girl was probably underage and a cop was watching him get into the car with her. The word "entrapment" or a close approximation thereof entered his head but he didn't have the ability to fight it.

He got into the passenger seat and looked at the girl crawling into the driver's seat and sliding it way forward. He had to close one eye to see her very well. She looked good. Vaguely familiar but he wasn't about to try and figure out where from. Small. Compact but nicely rounded body. Blond hair.

"Are you sure you're old enough to drive?" he asked.

She placed a finger over his lips. He was sure he was imagining it but he kind of thought the finger smelled like vagina.

He sat in the passenger seat and watched the town and then the country go by. He was wondering if this girl was taking him somewhere for sex and thought it was probably too good to be true. Given his masturbation session earlier and all the drinks he'd had at the bar, he wasn't even entirely sure he'd be able to get it up. He'd already forgotten that she'd asked him to be quiet a couple of times and so prepared to launch into his story about what he'd seen earlier, maybe it was remembering the masturbation that had made him think of it, when it finally hit him why this particular girl looked so familiar.

"So ..." Wayne suddenly felt a lot more sober. "My name's Wayne. What's yours?"

"Ilya."

That was the name of the villainess in *Vampires in Devil Town* so Wayne should have felt like he was somehow being put on. Being really drunk, having just received his largest royalties payment ever and therefore suffering a minor delusion of grandeur, he told himself, "Groupie."

"Where are we going, Ilya?" Wayne thought he knew. He was totally prepared to jump out of the car until he remembered this was exactly what he'd gone in search of.

"My place on Suchling Road."

"Ah."

Wayne pulled his phone out of his pocket. He anticipated a need for it. He flash forwarded to the future and had a vision of himself holding the phone in front of him and screaming into it like a girl.

It was dead.

Once he remembered they were in his car, he fished around in the dark until locating the charger cord and plugged it in.

He felt so many different things right now, but the overriding sensation was the stiffness of his cock in his pants.

He unfastened his seatbelt he didn't even remember buckling, leaned over in his seat, and began sloppily licking Ilya's ear. He felt her recoil and didn't know if that was a good thing or a bad thing.

"Do you think it's possible for a person to know something without having any idea they know anything?" she said.

Wayne thought this sounded extremely cryptic and out of place.

He removed his mouth from her ear and said, "I don't know. Why?"

She stopped the car in the middle of the road. It was a slow stop. She didn't slam on the brakes or anything. Still, it was an awkward thing to do. She put the car in park. As if on cue, it started to rain. An immediate feeling of isolation surrounded the car. Wayne thought he should be more afraid than he was. If he hadn't made a conscious decision to try and shut down the rational part of his brain, he probably would have been terrified.

"Are you looking for magic?"

"Magic? I don't know. I guess I'm looking for something."

Sitting there in the passenger seat of his own car, he felt very confused. This wasn't what he was expecting at all. He suddenly felt heavy and a little bit empty and his penis wilted in his pants.

"You've heard of the world behind this one?"

The girl, Ilya, turned her head toward him and he saw that her eyes were completely black. He didn't really know what she was asking him. Was she talking about his book? He could have asked her if she was talking about *Vampires in Devil Town* but he thought that would seem really presumptuous and egotistical. Instead, he decided to fight what might just be craziness with more craziness.

"I think I saw you earlier," he said.

"And why's that?"

"I was ... in the woods."

"And?"

Did she know? Did she know he'd been standing there just inside the woods and masturbating while she was getting fucked and bitten by one of those things? He felt strangely guilty.

"I saw you with that guy."

"He made me feel good. Complete."

"Complete?"

"He made me what I've always been. It was almost too easy. And what were you doing?"

Wayne kind of laughed.

"Show me," she said.

"Show you?"

"Show me exactly what you were doing while I was becoming."

Now Wayne's erection was back.

He cleared his throat. "No offense, but I'd rather actually fuck you."

She smiled, moved a hand over the bulge in his pants. "You and I are connected in ways you could never imagine."

The image of the villainess from his book popped into his head. What she said was no less cryptic than what she had been saying.

"So why do you want to watch me do that?"

"I like it. You watched me getting fucked. You watched me getting bitten. I think you owe it to me."

Wayne unbuttoned and unzipped his jeans, shucking them down with his underwear. His penis sprang up. He took it in his hand. She looked intently at his penis and he looked at those freaky black eyes.

"You tell stories," she said. "I have many stories to tell. Would you like to hear them?"

Wayne sat there, pumping his penis, wondering what the hell was going on. Things seemed to be getting stranger and stranger. Making no sense at all.

"Now?" he asked.

"We all have a function even if some people's function is to not have a function."

"I guess the world needs filler."

"Everyone has an individual story but it's very few people who can shape and influence the story of so many others. This town, Lynchville, is *my* story. Do you know what I'm saying?"

He didn't. Not really. And he was close to coming. He felt things warping and bending inside of him.

"I think maybe you haven't chosen which person you want to be yet."

Wayne felt like his brain was being attacked. He'd had his eyes closed and when he opened them again he looked at the window where he was expecting to see the rain beating down but it was covering it in black like ink was raining from the sky and he held himself in his hand but there was this girl sitting next to him and she was putting off this huge sexual vibe. At that point he thought maybe she was the most erotic female he'd ever encountered. He grabbed her arm and she didn't pull away. And then he was opening his door and pulling her across the seat and they were outside. The cold rain beat down and Wayne noted with relief that it wasn't black at all. It just had a way of turning the night black, turning the air to steam and now he had the girl in both hands and dragged her to the edge of the woods where he unbuttoned her pants and ripped them down. He forced her onto her back on a patch of grass and then he was between her legs, buried in her warmth and maybe crying and she whispered strange things he didn't understand into his ear. The only thing he did understand was her saying, "Bite me." She was giving him exactly what he wanted so he decided to return the favor. He bit her. Bit her until she bled.

Twenty-nine

When John finally came to, the sun was blinding him. He was outside. He had to reach back to think of the last thing he remembered. It had been so long since he'd woken anywhere except his house that he was completely confused.

He'd followed the screaming and the laughter to the strange house in the woods and ...

Melanie.

He'd fucked Melanie.

Then he'd bitten her.

Then he ... hadn't felt very well.

He'd gone back into the house to rest and had, he guessed, passed out.

So where was he now?

He stood up and still felt woozy. He braced himself on a nearby tree and fought the urge to vomit. Sweat broke out on his forehead and a shiver ran through him. He needed to get home. Shit. If it was the next day, that meant he'd missed Cassie's visit. And that meant she'd be pissed at him. It seemed like she was pissed at him a lot, anyway.

He looked around for the house he had presumably come from but didn't see anything. He was surrounded by woods. Thicker than anything he'd ever really seen around Lynchville.

He took a deep breath.

Shit.

It really was a gorgeous day. The air smelled almost sweet. There were so few days in Ohio that were perfect. Mainly the weather was good at being volatile. Otherwise it was just uncomfortably cold or grossly hot and humid.

Unless he wasn't in Ohio.

It seemed like a flippant thought but, walking through the unfamiliar woods, feeling them growing thicker and gloomier around him, the possible reality of that thought hit him. He'd never been here. No, he wasn't that lucky. The Devils had come for him for reasons he still wasn't too clear about. But he was sure Cassie *had* been here. She'd told him about it during the period they were trapped on the farm. She said she'd seen his brother, Elliot, in the dream. She said this place was called Neverly—the town behind the town. John was never quite sure how much of what Cassie said was fact and how much was supposition. He assumed everything she had been told had come from Elliot ... but maybe not the real Elliot. Maybe some dream Elliot that may not have been Elliot at all but a Devil impersonating him.

Reality seemed to be an increasingly tricky business in Lynchville.

Cassie had told him this other place, Neverly, was where the Devils hid. There were some who actively took over people in the real world. There were those who existed in the real world as mostly spirits—ghosts—and were ultimately harmless. Those two levels represented the most evolved states of the Devils. The bulk of them were monsters. Monsters waiting for the door between our world and theirs to open so they could rush out and feast on human blood and flesh until there wasn't any left.

Monsters.

And there was a distinct possibility he could be in their territory now.

Monsters.

Just like him, he thought. He was a monster. Everyone else seemed to know this about him. He could understand Cassie thinking he was a monster. He could understand the rest of the townsfolk thinking he was a monster for potentially killing his parents. But Melanie had known, too. Known the truth. If she had known, how many other people did? Why hadn't *he* known?

But he had, he guessed, to be fair to himself. He'd known ever since being trapped on his farm, stalking Cassie like prey. He just hadn't wanted to believe it.

And now he'd made Melanie a monster, too. Well, maybe not a complete monster. One had to also drink the blood of a Devil to become what they were. But a bite from them would certainly send them on their way. It would make her exactly what he was, since he had never partaken of Devil blood.

Once again he stopped in his tracks.

If he *were* in Neverly, that would mean he had the power to go back and forth. That was something he hadn't had the power to do before, not that he'd tried.

But Cassie said she'd been there.

No. That wasn't necessarily true. Cassie had said she'd seen it because Elliot showed it to her. Meaning he could have just as easily given her a vision.

Somewhere in the distance, he again heard that laughing scream. Now he couldn't even tell which one it was.

He thought he should probably just turn around and go back the way he'd come. But he was here and he was curious and he wasn't really sure he had anything to go back to.

No. That wasn't true. He did know what he was going back to. Melanie.

He had turned her. Whether he was happy with that decision or not, it was one he'd made. He turned a girl who he'd only known a few minutes instead of turning Cassie.

Why not Cassie?

Was it because she never specifically asked him to and it would have been too much like rape if he'd done it without her permission? Or was it because it really was a kind of death, whether either of them wanted o admit it or not, and Cassie seemed too young and full of life to do that to? Or was it something else? Was it because he knew they were doomed and had been for a while?

Now John had convinced himself he was just walking to clear his head. It was probably ridiculous to think he was anywhere other than the real world anyway. He could do that as much as he wanted to. Sometimes he just had to admit to himself he wasn't the sanest, most rational person on the planet.

In the near distance, he caught a brief glimpse of movement, like a person moving away from him. Of course it could just as easily have been a butterfly or a bird.

He followed the movement.

He was suddenly aware of the wind rustling the trees and the birds chirping around him and the clean natural smells of the woods. He didn't see how he could be anywhere but the real world.

Thirty

Cassie awoke to an empty bed. She was mad at Melanie but couldn't remember exactly why. She kicked the covers from her naked body and stretched. She was sore. Everywhere sore. Her muscles ached, but so did her jaws and between her legs and even her ass. But thinking of how she'd become so sore brought nothing but pleasant memories.

Maybe she was just upset Melanie wasn't here now.

Then she remembered.

The bite mark.

Cassie wasn't going to come right out and question Melanie. Things with her were still in the early stages and, if she were wrong, she didn't want to do anything to drive her away. But she could and would question John about it. She thought he owed her something. After all, she'd been his daily dinner for over a year now. If he was just going to toss her aside, then she thought she deserved to know.

That seemed really hypocritical. And probably not necessarily true. The reality of it had more to do with her no longer being afraid to lose John but wanting to hang on to Melanie. If anything, he was the one who deserved answers.

And what if it was true?

What if he had bitten Melanie? Turned her?

What then?

That would mean the two most important people in her life besides her parents were Devils.

Maybe then she should just have one of them turn her too so they could live as a big, happy threesome.

And, she thought, wouldn't that actually make her truly happy?

Everything seemed moot without first getting some answers.

She got out of bed and tried to stretch away some of the stiffness before taking a shower and heading out to John's.

Thirty-one

Wayne woke up in a ditch for not the first time in his life. He was soaking wet but, luckily, it was warm outside. He stood up and reached for his phone in his pocket. Its absence incited a brief, blinding moment of panic. He took a few deep breaths and tried to clear his head. The missing phone was probably not the most horrible thing that had happened to him last night. He had a terrible taste in his mouth and it felt like someone was pinching his ears.

First things first ...

He climbed out of the ditch.

Parts of last night were still with him. He remembered that freaky girl and leaving his car in the middle of the road.

His car was no longer in the middle of the road. It was nowhere to be seen.

Jesus. His ears *hurt*. He raised his hands to massage them or something and discovered he had a rubber band wrapped around his head. He pulled it off, taking some hair with it, and realized the rubber band was there to hold a note in place.

Only it wasn't a note.

It was a parking ticket.

Which meant he wasn't as finished with the Lynchville Police Department as much as both parties would have wished. He almost decided to say fuck it and leave his car there but his phone was probably in it. He didn't think he really had the money to get the car out. He *did* have the money, but he was hoping to use it for something more important, like drinking. Maybe they would let him get his possessions out of it. All he had to do was think back to his one encounter with Chief Bowsman to reassure himself that probably wasn't happening.

"Fuck," he mumbled.

He began walking back to town before he could talk himself out of it. It gave him some time to reflect on the previous night. All in all, he'd have to say it went well. He had opened his senses and his imagination to the reality of the Devils and he was pretty sure one of them picked him up. He was also pretty sure he'd had sex with her. Evil being or not, that was a plus. In fact, Wayne would have considered every woman he'd ever had sex with to be an evil being. Then he had bitten her. That was cause for concern. He knew AIDS medication had gotten pretty good, so that wasn't really what he was worried about. But if she *had* been a Devil, and he'd drunk her blood, it seemed like something inside of him should be changing.

Thinking that seemed to open some kind of paranoid rabbit hole his mind quickly spiraled down into. Maybe he shouldn't be walking to the police station. Last night, he'd thought things seemed a little too easy. He'd even considered entrapment. Meaning that if the cops had been close enough to give him a ticket for leaving his car on the road, then they may have also been nearby while he was fucking what was most probably a minor.

He looked at the ticket again, not really knowing what he expected to find. The words "Statutory Rape" in the violation line, maybe? Or some vaguely accusatory slant to the handwriting. He stopped and mumbled, "Fuck," again.

He heard a car behind him and quickly turned around.

He really was paranoid. He expected it to be a cop. He'd made the split second decision to take off running if it was.

It wasn't a cop but it did slow down as it drew closer to him. And as it pulled up beside him, Wayne saw the girl from last night.

Potentially good.

Potentially really bad.

"Hi!" she said. She seemed really cheerful and smiley.

"Uh ... hi," Wayne said.

"Hop in."

Wayne wasn't sure if that was a good idea. He moved closer to the car to see what the girl thought—good idea or bad.

"Come on," she said. "Hop in. I don't bite." He crossed in front of the car and thought he heard her say, "Unlike you."

He pulled the door handle and it was locked so he panicked and just kept pulling on it like a child. Finally it unlocked and he collapsed into the passenger seat.

"Rough night?" the girl asked. Wayne felt really bad that he couldn't remember her name but she was acting like she didn't remember anything.

"Kind of," he said. "Somebody left me on the side of the road."

"I left your car with you. I left the keys in the ignition and everything."

Wayne held the ticket up in front of her.

"Oh. Oops."

"Yeah. Oops. I don't think I'm going to go pick it up."

"I can take you."

He waved her off. "Say, you don't know if anyone happened to see us together last night, do you?"

"What? You mean like the cop who gave you the ticket?"

"Exactly."

"And you're worried about that because I'm underage?"

"So acute."

"I don't think so. Let me take you to pick up your car. It's the least I can do."

"No. What happened last night isn't the only reason. It goes back a couple of days. But I'm pretty sure I can't go the police station yet. You don't happen to have a phone I could borrow, do you?"

She reached into her pocket and pulled out her phone, handing it over to him. He stared at it and said, "Can you get the Internet on this?"

She pressed a button at the bottom and a browser popped up.

"Thank God," he said.

"Why do you need it?"

"I left my phone in the car. I have insurance on it. This way I can get them to send me a new one without having to go to a police station."

"Wow. That's really ... brave."

"Thanks. I'm going to tell them it exploded while I was talking on it."

"And honest, too."

"But you could do me a huge favor and take me home so I can put some clean clothes on."

"Where's home?"

He directed her.

Thirty-two

John continued to track the movement he'd seen earlier. He still had no idea if he was in the real world or that other place. He kind of felt like he was sliding back and forth. The woods here were definitely denser than anything he'd ever seen in Lynchville. Not only did there seem to be more of them, they seemed taller. So if he was still in Lynchville, it was some area he'd never been in. Which wasn't entirely impossible. It wasn't like he'd ever been much for exploring. But he figured he would still be somewhere around his house and that was an area where he thought he'd seen everything.

He watched the movement as it crossed a clearing in front of him. Now he was pretty sure it was a figure. Female probably. In the brief second he was able to track her, he thought it looked like she wore a white gown. He thought about calling out to her but he wanted a better idea of where she was going first.

And what was he going to say to her if he did catch up with her? Ask her where he was? He could imagine himself looking even crazier than everyone already thought he was.

He was getting ahead of himself. He thought he was doing a

pretty good job of staying calm. Not that panicking would have helped anything. At least tracking the figure was giving him something to do, giving him some measure of forward momentum. The last thing he needed to do was stand in one place and think about things.

Just as he thought about continuous movement, he heard the screaming laughter again. This time it sounded really close. Now he stood in the clearing, ready to follow in the direction of the girl, but he stopped to see if he could find the source of that sound.

As he stood there, the sound seemed to move closer and closer to him, deafening. Not just deafening—piercing and painful, like it was punching holes in his equilibrium. From the middle of the clearing, he watched the trees spin around him. And every second, he caught a glimpse of the figure moving away from him. Farther and farther every time that part of his vision spun back around.

Unable to remain upright, he collapsed into the middle of the clearing with no idea what was happening to him.

Thirty-three

Cassie pulled up in front of John's half-expecting to see Melanie's car already there. She still didn't know exactly how to feel if that happened. She knew how she would react. Probably with blind rage. Her reaction to a lot of things lately. But, as quick to anger as she sometimes was, she still considered herself to be a mostly rational person. Sometimes it just took her a bit of time and distance to figure things out.

It didn't look like Melanie was there. She got out of the car and walked toward the front door. She figured John would be there. If her supposition was correct and he and Melanie *were* together yesterday, it would have to have been while she was at work. Probably right before she got off if John still hadn't made it home by the time she got there. That would have given him plenty of time to get back. Even if he and Melanie *hadn't* been together and he'd just gone off somewhere to sulk, then he would definitely be there.

She knocked and went into the house. Called for him. Still nothing.

Wandering around the house, Cassie didn't see any signs of him being there at all. The book he'd been reading still rested open, pages down on the coffee table. The air felt stale. Like he hadn't been there to take a shower or open the door to come and go or anything.

If he was still avoiding her, she thought it had to be more out of guilt than anger.

Of course, she thought, no one but her knew the things she thought she knew. As for John and Melanie, it was entirely possible that both of them thought she was completely ignorant about everything.

She pulled out her phone to call Melanie. She still wasn't sure if she should ask her anything about John so she figured she would just try and rope Melanie into doing something to make sure she and John were not somewhere together.

"Hello?" It was a man's voice and for a heart stopping moment Cassie thought it was John. She couldn't force any words out.

"Hello? Speak."

Speak? She almost laughed for thinking it could be John. He was way too polite to talk like that on the phone.

"Um, hi, I might have the wrong number."

"Who is this?"

"Cassie."

"Hi, Cassie, this is Wayne. Were you trying to reach ...?"

"Melanie."

"Hm."

An awkward amount of time passed. She heard him say, "Melanie?" like he was terminally confused, before she heard Melanie's voice.

"Cassie?"

"Yeah. Who was that?"

"Wayne."

"Wayne?"

"Yep."

"Who's Wayne?"

"Some guy I'm giving a ride."

"You picked up a hitchhiker?"

"Well, I thought he looked familiar, like one of my dad's friends and by the time I stopped and realized I didn't know him I was afraid I'd gotten his hopes up and didn't want to just leave him stranded."

"Okay. Hey, did you want to do something today?"

"Sure. Like what?"

"I don't know. Maybe help me look for John."

"I thought you were about done with that guy."

"He's still not home. I'm kind of worried. Help me look for him and, when he turns up, I promise I'll talk to him. Okay?"

"Okay. I'll be there in about a half an hour. Did you wanna talk to Wayne again?"

"What? No!"

Melanie laughed and hung up.

Cassie lay down on the couch and wished she had something to drink.

Thirty-four

Ilya knew the man sitting next to her had already forgotten her name. At first, she was slightly offended by this, but when he'd decided to take it upon himself to answer the phone when Cassie called, she was glad. Sometimes, especially if the host person was remarkably similar to whom Ilya had originally been, it was difficult to remember that, to everyone else, she *was* that person. Not Ilya.

This was her second encounter with Wayne Hixon. Both of them were something like planned accidents. She had a way of *influencing* things but she couldn't directly make anyone do anything unless it was through brute force. She didn't know about Wayne. She knew he'd written a book called *Vampires in Devil Town* about a town called Lynchville that was remarkably similar to this Lynchville. It was a work of fiction and not many people had read it. But it had the potential to be really dangerous. As many of her kind were spread across the globe, there were even more people who would like to see her kind destroyed. Many of them used to operate through churches but most churches were beginning to see any study of the occult—even if the overall outcome was intended to be "good"—as evil. So most of the people who would like to see the Devils pushed back into their own world or destroyed altogether operated on their own or in very small societies. Those were the people she was afraid of seeing the book. They knew what to look out for. They had destroyed many of her kind, a lot of them more powerful than she was. All they would have to do is some minor research into this Hixon guy's background, find out where he had come from, study some history, and the somewhat blatant patterns spelled out there, and they would be here.

Luckily, Hixon was lazy and wasn't easily researchable. The biography in the back of the book was mostly a lie and his publisher seemed to be mostly unresponsive to contact.

She couldn't figure out if Hixon had intended to write such an exposé or if he was some kind of idiot savant. He seemed to be guided only by rage and his dick. Even now he sat in the passenger seat staring at her crotch and rubbing his thighs. Surely he didn't think she couldn't see him.

So she was torn. She didn't want to let him live, but if he mysteriously disappeared, that might stimulate more questions about him. Okay, maybe not *more* questions, since there hadn't really been any inquiries that she knew.

Her immediate plan was to keep him close. He seemed kind of cowardly so she thought his only weapon was probably a pen and paper.

Not that it would matter in a couple of days anyway.

Her only human obstacles were John and Cassie. Particularly, it seemed, John and Cassie together. John was one of them. He'd been born to be one of them. Unfortunately, that made him essential to bringing Neverly to Lynchville. Once that happened, they could begin building their society of Devils and spreading out quicker than they ever had. However, as long as Cassie was alive, that wasn't going to happen. It didn't even matter that they were no longer in love like they had been the first time. It was now almost a more dangerous kind of love. Cassie was John's protector. Whether she wanted to be or not, she wouldn't let anything happen to John if she could help it. Luckily for Ilya, Cassie lived in the world where there was a whole array of things to distract her from what was, perhaps, her supreme purpose in life.

Now Ilya was meeting Cassie later. That gave her a small amount of time to think about what she could do to her.

Hixon was another matter altogether. She'd tried to pull some of this information—about how much he actually *knew* about doing what he was doing—but he seemed mostly incoherent. If he truly didn't know that his job was to document the happenings in Lynchville, that made him an almost bigger threat. Basically, she needed to keep him from being in the right places at the right times. Already, just since he'd returned, he'd witnessed John's first transformation since his initiate period, as well as John turning who he thought was Melanie, and Ilya fully turning John into a very powerful Devil. God only knew what else he'd seen.

She pulled up his driveway and stopped in front of his house.

He looked dazed or maybe just stupid. He started to get out and she grabbed his hand, pulled him close to her, and kissed him deeply.

"I'd like to see you tonight," she said.

"Uh, okay."

"Meet me in front of Nilbog's again?"

"Um ... I have to walk?"

"Would you rather I pick you up here?"

"Sure. I'd really like to take a shower."

She paused and looked inward. Accessed the rough road map of Melanie that was left. Saturday. Sunday. Summer. A cabin on a lake in Tennessee. Of course, her parents were there. Had probably left sometime yesterday afternoon.

She smiled. "I can take you back to my place and you can grab a shower."

"Wouldn't your parents mind?"

"They're out of town. But I've got some things I need to do so I might have to leave you there alone. Is that okay?"

"That's fine. Can I run in here and grab some freshish clothes?"

"Sure. Actually, you can do some wash at my place too. Just don't leave anything behind."

"Thanks." Hixon got out of the car and headed toward the blackened shell of his house.

Poor sap. Ilya knew the best way to keep a man out of trouble was to give him a list of chores and the prospect of sex.

Thirty-five

John came to even more confused than he had been when he'd gone out. Melanie's face hovering over him made it that much more confusing.

"Melanie?" His mouth felt really dry, coated in something gross. While he didn't eat people food, he did drink water and, very occasionally, wine. Those were the only things he could keep down.

"We need to get you out of here."

"Where is here? And why are you here?"

"It's terrible, John. I'm so sorry."

"Sorry for what? I'm the one who bit you. Maybe even used you. I'm the one who should be sorry."

"No. I'll explain later. Can you stand up?"

John stood up slowly, fearing the worst. He still felt bad but nothing like he'd felt before. This felt manageable. And now, with some vague promise of answers, he felt the need to get up. Melanie grabbed his hand and started pulling him in the direction she had been going. That was assuming she was the figure he'd been following. He didn't really see any alternative.

"Where are we going?" he asked.

"We need to find a way to get you back to Lynchville. You don't want to be here after dark."

"Where are we?"

"Neverly."

"How ...?"

"I think I know."

He was hoping she would tell him but she didn't say anything. Maybe she wanted to get wherever it was she was going before she told him anything.

"Where are you taking me?"

"My house. Or a version of it, anyway."

"I'm kind of freaked out."

"Shh ... You're going to want to save your energy."

They continued through the woods and, gradually, John noticed other shapes in the distance. City shapes. Or small town shapes, anyway. It looked a lot like Lynchville but it could have been any other small town in America. Of course, from this distance, it seemed more ... slouching. He noticed other things, too. How Melanie's hand felt cold against his. How, while he had broken a sweat in the heat of the day, she didn't have a droplet of moisture anywhere on her. And how, while his breathing was deep and nearly ragged, he couldn't hear anything coming from her.

Melanie was dead. She hadn't even become a Devil. She was a victim. Trapped here. He wondered if it was his fault. He *never* would have bitten her if he thought that would happen.

They exited the woods and entered the cemetery. The tombstones leaned every which way, many of them cracked and broken. Piles of earth were in front of many of the stores, as though the corpses had either clawed their way out or been harvested by someone on the surface. The bad feeling John had had since the first time he'd come to was intensified. He felt it pressing on his chest. Melanie led him through the cemetery with her cold hand. He thought she lived close to Cassie, which meant they were relatively close to her house if this *was* a kind of mirror of

Lynchville.

So far it seemed like it was but everything was either more intensified or more decimated.

The row houses at his end of the town were crumbling. All the windows had been shattered. It looked like some of them had been burned. The sidewalks were mostly nonexistent. The roads were broken and potholed, grass and shrubbery growing up between the asphalt.

Yet, despite the appearance of this other town, it was quiet and, if it hadn't been for that feeling of dread deep in his viscera, John would have found it somewhat peaceful. No cars. No people. No planes. It reminded him of a documentary he'd seen that showed what would happen when the human race was wiped off the face of the earth and nature was able to run rampant.

He stopped. He felt the urge to take it all in.

"It's kind of ... pretty," he said.

Melanie tugged on him. "There's no time."

They veered out of town and onto a tree-lined suburban street. The trees looked blighted. Branches hung from them, too low to the ground. Massive cocoons possibly housing some kind of worm or parasite enshrouded much of them. John had never seen anything like it.

Then Melanie was leading him up a smashed driveway. The front yard featured a massive hole. Hanging from the front door was a dried out corpse, adorned in shredded and mildewed outdated clothing. Melanie pulled the door open and they went into the stinking house. John couldn't specifically identify the stink. It was sort of like every bad smell in the world had convened to form some stench that was nearly palpable. If he hadn't been living off blood for the past year, he might have gagged.

"And we're ... safe here?"

"Safer," Melanie said. "We're not *safe* anywhere here. You might not be safe anywhere."

John knew what this meant. He nearly predicted what she said before she actually said it.

"She's come back."

The terrible feeling John had had was nothing compared to this moment. He closed his eyes and lowered his head.

"And?" he said.

"You're part of her now. She owns you."

"How?"

"I'm not sure of the specifics. I ... there are some things I need to tell you. I can make it quick."

John felt like he wanted to sit down but he didn't want to sit anywhere here.

"I was the one leaving offerings for you but maybe you already knew that. I'm not sure why you were at the house but that was where we did most of the sacrifices—"

"We?"

"I had some help but that's nothing to worry about. They were mostly sheep."

"So was it *human* blood?"

She lowered her head, looked ashamed. "Every time except for the first time."

"Jesus, Melanie."

"Not so important now. The last thing I remember was going to that house because I had a feeling I'd forgotten to do something."

"Do something?"

"Yeah, like clean-up or whatever, even though I've never worried about that before. And then I remember getting there and seeing you and then things started to get cloudy."

"How so?"

"Because *she* had moved into me."

"Moved into you?"

"Don't act so surprised. You know what they're capable of. So there's a period where I remember some things but I had to fight for control of what I was saying and had absolutely no control over what I was doing."

"So you don't remember ..."

"No. That's why I'm able to tell you this. I remember fucking. That person who took over my body made me do that even though she hated every second of it. I wanted you to turn me, but I didn't want that. What I said about me and Cassie was true. We've been together for a while. I love ... loved her a lot. And that person who was inside me wanted you to bite her so you could drink her blood."

"Thus completing the process."

"I'm afraid she's going to hurt Cassie, John."

"Why would she want to do that?"

"Because you and Cassie are meant to be together. Maybe not necessarily as a couple but definitely as a team. Cassie's told me about your history. You've defeated this bitch before and you were together."

John didn't know what to say. He closed his eyes and put his hands over his face. He felt trapped. Hopeless. Now he would have to rally everything he had and go after the Devils again. Only he felt like it was pointless. They already thought they'd killed her once before and now she was back. She'd already tricked him and now it sounded like she was going to go after Cassie. If Melanie loved Cassie and Cassie felt the same way about her, then Ilya had found the perfect Trojan horse. And he had to figure out a way to get out of Neverly.

Suddenly Melanie looked around the room, her eyes wide, and said, "She knows I'm here."

"What? What does that mean?"

But even as he said that Melanie began ... breaking up in front of him. Separating into tendrils of blue mist and then gone. In her place was something that looked like a bag of meat on the floor. Or maybe it was a skinned, legless dog. It twitched and made a strange keening noise. John rushed to the front door and outside.

It was dark.

<h1 align="center">Thirty-six</h1>

While lying on the couch waiting for Melanie and thinking about things, Cassie had let her righteous anger build. She liked Melanie a lot. She'd decided to confront her first thing. If they had any hope of making this last, they had to be honest with each other. Cassie felt like she had been nothing but honest with Melanie and, if Melanie had been doing what Cassie thought she had been doing, then that meant she had been lied to continuously. It almost made her reconsider her feelings completely.

There was a gentle knock on the door.

Cassie crossed the room and opened the door, her blood pumping furiously.

Melanie stood in the doorway looking sweet and innocent.

"Come in," Cassie said. "Sit down."

Melanie crossed the room and sat down on the couch. Cassie stood in front of her and, half to combat the urge to kiss Melanie, she reached out and smacked her on the face as hard as she could.

"How could you?"

Melanie slowly brought her head back around. A handprint was already reddening on her cheek. Tears welled at the corners of her eyes.

"How could I ... what?"

"Please stop lying to me." Now Cassie was crying, half out of anger, half out of frustration.

"I don't know what you—"

But Cassie had already reached out and grabbed a handful of her hair. She pushed Melanie's face into the couch and hopped on her back. She yanked the neckline of her t-shirt down and started jabbing furiously at the bite mark.

"This! This! This! How can you explain that? What have you been doing with John? Was it you who left the offerings? Was it animal blood or have you been killing people, Melanie?"

Beneath Cassie, Melanie turned over onto her back. Melanie was the smaller of the two but she put her hands on Cassie and pushed. It was the shove of a bodybuilder. Cassie went over the edge of the couch. Melanie was up and on her in a second. Cassie had never seen anyone move that fast. Now Melanie was on top of her, leaning into her, and Cassie noticed the eyes.

All black.

No whites anywhere.

And Cassie felt like that was all the proof she needed. She thought she felt her heart break with one final sob.

"Why did you let him do that?" she said.

"Is that really what you mean? Or do you mean why did I *want* him to do it? And why did he do it so readily? Maybe because his girlfriend wouldn't have any part of it? Maybe because he knew you would grow apart."

"Oh, Melanie," Cassie sobbed.

Now Melanie pressed herself down on Cassie. She put her hands on her breasts, ground her hips into her crotch. "Cassie, let me turn you. Please. You know how great it would be. We'd have each other forever. You could have John, too."

Cassie almost got lost in those eyes. Melanie lowered her head to Cassie's neck and just that close proximity sent something like an electrical charge from her neck to her crotch. For a brief second, she was going to let her do anything she wanted to do but ... something didn't seem right. She tried to push Melanie off, but Melanie moved her hands from Cassie's breasts to her wrists and slammed them to the floor above her head. A string of drool ran from Melanie's mouth, landing on Cassie's chin.

"No, Mel ..."

"Maybe you don't have a choice."

"This isn't what I want."

Melanie moved her head closer to Cassie's neck again, whispered in her ear, "You never know what you want, do you?"

Melanie opened her mouth and Cassie saw the fangs inside. John had been a Devil way longer than Melanie and, as far as Cassie knew, he wasn't able to do that yet. Something definitely wasn't right. Cassie slammed her head into Melanie's face. The other girl's grip broke just long enough to allow Cassie to roll out from underneath her. She stood up and said, "Where's John?"

Melanie lay on the floor, wiping blood from her mouth with the back of her hand and laughing.

Thirty-seven

Wayne guessed her name was Melanie. That was what the girl on the phone had called her and that's what she had answered to, so that was probably proof enough. But it still didn't seem right to Wayne. He was pretty sure she'd given him her name last night and Melanie didn't ring any bells at all.

After picking him up, Melanie had swung by his house so he could get some clothes. Then she took him back to her house. Wayne was secretly hoping for a quickie but, today, she seemed completely disinterested in sex. Once she left, he felt kind of like Goldilocks in her house. The house was nice so he wasn't disappointed when he found the liquor cabinet. He poured a couple fingers of Macallan's and pounded it. That cleared out his head a little bit. He took his bag of clothes into the laundry room and jammed the washer as full as he possibly could. Back in Illinois, where he'd mostly had a job, he just dropped his clothes off at a laundromat. He made the washing machine make sounds and figured he'd done something right. He went to the bathroom and realized he hadn't brought any clean clothes. Since he was the only one here, he didn't figure it really mattered much. After taking a very long, very hot shower, and using most of the various cleansers and shampoos in the shower, he dried off and wrapped a fresh towel around his fleshy waist.

Time to revisit the liquor cabinet, he thought.

This time he filled the glass half full of the scotch and downed it in a couple of gulps. He made himself comfortable on the leather couch and turned on the TV. It was on Fox News and he felt a second of rage before he flipped to a less offensive news channel. He supposed the news should have made him feel like part of the world but, sitting there in a posh home in Lynchville, he couldn't have felt more removed.

It didn't take long for him to fall asleep.

Thirty-eight

John felt even more lost without Melanie. She had warned him against the dark but he didn't see anything overtly threatening. He had no idea what he was supposed to do or where he was supposed to go. He knew he needed to get back but didn't know how he was supposed to do that. Plus, despite drinking so much of Melanie's blood yesterday, he was incredibly hungry. Of course, if what she said was true, then it wasn't really her he'd bitten at all, but Ilya. And that was bad news.

If there had been any going back before, there definitely wasn't now.

He wasn't sure what that meant.

Familiarity still meant something to him so he started for Cassie's house. She only lived one street over. He didn't really expect to find anything there. It was only about a ten minute walk. It was quiet. He would have thought "too quiet" but, growing up on a farm, there really wasn't such a thing. Her house had the same hollowed out, devastated look the rest of the houses had. He didn't think it was necessary to knock on the door. The inside didn't seem as disgusting as Melanie's but he thought that might only be because there wasn't any light streaming in through the windows. The stink was definitely not as pungent, though there was still an odor.

He considered turning around and leaving, heading back the way he'd come. If there was some kind of doorway into this world and he had made it here, it stood to reason he could find that doorway again.

Unless Ilya was the doorway.

Maybe it was her blood that had sent him here.

Maybe that was what being a Devil was all about. Maybe they did exist but the legends and rumors were all just that. Maybe the only way they had of infecting the people of Lynchville was through dreams.

And if he *was* a Devil, then he didn't really think he would have a lot to be afraid of anyway.

He was at the front door, ready to leave, when he heard that screaming laugh again. Although now it was more of a sob. It sounded like it came from somewhere upstairs. Extremely familiar with this house, he found the stairs and climbed them.

He heard the sobbing again. It came from one of the bedrooms at the end of the hall. The one Cassie's dad used for an office.

John's defenses were up and he had to pause a second to realize what that meant. When changed, his body was a weapon with claws, teeth, strength. He felt like he could change instantly if threatened. He pushed open the door.

A small girl sat on the floor, crying.

She held Cassie's head in her lap.

A man John had never seen before stood in the corner of the room alternately masturbating and beating his chest.

"This isn't my mommy." The little girl dropped Cassie's head on the floor. The man in the corner rushed over, scooped up the head, took it back into the corner, and began fucking its rotten mouth.

"Will you help me find my mommy?" The girl held out a hand to John.

He knew he had to at least get her out of the room and away from this man. He pulled her up to her feet, left the room, and shut the door.

"Thanks," she said. "That man was really bothering me."

John wasn't sure what this meant and didn't think he wanted to know.

"Do you know where your mom is?" he asked her, as gently and softly as he could.

"I think she's in the woods with the others."

"The others?"

"Yep."

"Who are the others?"

"People like me and mommy. People who can't go home anymore."

Of course, John thought. Already, he was almost seduced by this world. This girl was probably no more real than Melanie had been. No more real than Cassie's head. It was this world's way of getting under his skin.

But, since he'd been planning on going that direction himself anyway, he said, "I'll take you to the woods and we can look for your mommy."

"Gee, thanks." The girl gave him a hug around his neck.

Even though she probably didn't exist, he still liked the feeling it gave him.

<h1 style="text-align:center">Thirty-nine</h1>

"Where is he!" Cassie shouted.

Melanie sprang to her feet in a maneuver Cassie was sure Melanie wasn't capable of.

"I can show you," Melanie said.

"What happened?"

"I've already told you. John bit me. He made me just like him."

"No. John was never like you."

"Maybe you don't know who I am."

"Melanie?" Cassie said.

Melanie shook her head. Blood still trickled from her mouth.

"Ilya?"

Ilya nodded her head. Melanie's head. Ilya's head now.

Cassie clutched her head with both of her hands. Not for the first time, she felt like she'd lost everything. John was nowhere to be found. He was probably in danger somewhere, if Ilya had anything to do with him not being here. And if Ilya now inhabited Melanie's body it meant Melanie was dead. Her spirit had been devoured by the witch inside of her body. That left Cassie with nothing. She just wanted to walk away and turn her back on everything.

Ilya glided toward her.

"You can have him," Cassie said.

Ilya stopped.

"We beat you before. I can't fight you again. Take him. Leave me the fuck alone."

For a moment, Ilya looked like she was considering this. Then she said, "I'm afraid it's not that simple."

"What do you mean it's not that simple? John's the only one who can bring your world here. You need him. I stood in your way before. Now I'm letting you have him. There. It's done."

Ilya lowered her head and said, "I don't forget things that easily."

"Well maybe you should start."

"No. You still have to pay."

Ilya sprang forward, throwing her weight on Cassie and driving her to the ground. Her mouth was on Cassie's neck, her teeth sinking into the soft flesh. Once her teeth were locked in, Cassie didn't even bother fighting.

She didn't know if Ilya was trying to turn her, to force her into a life of damnation, or if she was trying to kill her.

Cassie let it happen.

She felt herself grow weaker. She didn't know what the outcome would be and wasn't sure she cared.

Forty

When Wayne finally came to he stood in the kitchen, naked, shouting, "Attacked by a dog! Attacked by a dog! Hurry! Hurry!"

"Sir. Stop shouting. We have someone on the way."

"Not here!"

"I know, sir. You gave us the address. Let me also remind you that it's illegal to place false calls."

Wayne slammed the phone down. It didn't break or anything. They didn't make them like that anymore. He had no idea what that call or conversation was about. He felt out of his head. The towel was on the floor, around his feet, and he decided to leave it there. It was probably the last thing he needed, but he went back to the liquor cabinet and finished off the bottle of scotch. Then he went to the toilet and vomited. Then he sat on the toilet and had a great and smelly shit. Then he decided this house was doing something to fuck with his head even though it was probably the most normal house he'd ever been in and he grabbed his sopping wet clothes out of the washer, put them on, and left the rest of them there.

He stepped outside to the careening wail of sirens.

Forty-one

Ilya felt Cassie's life leaking away. Maybe there would have been easier ways to kill her, but this was how Ilya wanted to do it.

She stood up and looked down at Cassie, at the blood flowing out of her neck and pooling on the floor. Cassie's eyes were still open to slits.

Ilya heard the sirens in the distance. They were growing closer. Then they were in front of the house.

Ilya thought about finishing Cassie off and then thought better of it. The bitch was a goner. Let her have a second to think she might live, might pull through. Hell, let her go to the hospital. Let her parents get their hopes up. Let the whole thing be as dramatic as possible. And then let her die. Ilya wasn't going anywhere. If she was still alive tonight, Ilya would find her room and wouldn't leave until she was dead.

But for now she had to get the hell out of here.

As she ran out the back door, she heard the front door splinter.

Forty-two

They left Cassie's Neverly house. The little girl wouldn't let John not hold her hand. They stepped onto the decimated street and began walking back toward the edge of town.

"So what's your name?" John asked.

"Linda. What's yours?"

"My name's John."

"Oh."

"Oh?"

"It's kind of boring."

"Linda's not that great either."

"I know. But mostly I like to be called Panther."

John laughed. "Panther?"

"Yeah. They're beautiful. Like big kitty cats only ... *ferocious*." Linda growled the last word.

"I guess you're right about that."

"Do you have another name?"

"I have a middle name and a last name but I'm afraid I don't have a name as good as 'Panther'."

"That's okay. We can't all be panthers. Just me. That's the way I like it. All the other panthers are really far away and if I were to ever find them, I wouldn't be special anymore."

"You *are* special."

"Thanks. I know. Do you like it here?"

"Well, I haven't really been here all that long. Do *you* like it here?"

"I love it. I think it's beautiful."

"Really?"

"Uh huh. You'll see."

"Well, to tell you the truth. I'm kind of trying to leave."

"Why would you want to do that?"

"I have some people I need to get back to."

"Like I'm trying to get to my mommy?"

"Exactly. If I help you find your mom, do you think you could help me get back to where I need to go?"

The girl laughed quietly. "I guess that depends on where you need to go."

John tried to figure out how to explain it to her. He followed a hunch. "Do you remember dying?"

"What do you mean?"

"Well, remember when you lived in a house with your mom and dad and maybe some brothers and sisters and everything didn't look all old and broken and you got up to go to school and things?"

"Kind of."

"And then something happened and one day you were here."

"Yeah, Mommy wrecked the car and some nice people brought us here after they cleaned the blood off and everything." She paused, laughed, and said, "They cleaned it off with their *mouths*. It tickled. But Daddy and my brother Pete didn't come with us."

"Okay. So, do you know where they are now?"

"I do but I don't think I could get to them."

"That's where I need to go. So I want you to do me a favor and think really hard, okay? Think of how you would get to them and if anything comes to mind, you let me know. Okay?"

"Deal."

"Deal."

He shook her hand that he'd been holding. She complained about being tired of walking and he picked her up. After she told him how much she liked piggyback rides, he shifted her around to his back.

"So how long have you been here?"

"A very long time."

"What do you do?"

"Play, mostly."

"Play?"

"Sure."

"What do you play with?"

"Ha ha. People, of course."

"People?"

"Sleeping people."

"How do you do that?"

"Um, it's too hard to explain."

"Try. I think that's a really neat way to play with people."

Linda giggled again. "It is if you're *nice*. Some people aren't so nice. Some people are *mean*."

"So are you going to tell me how you do it?"

"I'll try."

"Shoot."

"Bang bang."

Now John laughed, more to put Linda at ease than anything else. He really didn't feel that much like laughing. "I mean try and *tell me* how you play with sleeping people."

"Okay but it's not like I'm really playing with the people who are sleeping ..."

"You mean you don't hold their eyes open or tickle their feet or anything?"

"Nooo . I couldn't do that. But maybe I could make them *think*

I'm doing that. I guess it's like I'm playing with their ..."

"Thoughts?"

"Maybe. But not all the time. They have to be asleep so ..."

"You're playing with their *dreams*?"

"*Yeah*! I'm giving them dreams."

"And some people give them ..."

"Nightmares."

"But not you. Because you're sweet and nice and stuff."

"The sweetest."

"So what's it like? Do you have to go somewhere to play or can you do it anywhere?"

"Um ..."

"Um? What?"

"I'm afraid I'll get in trouble if I tell you."

"That's silly. Why would you get in trouble?"

"Because sometimes we have to do bad things. I don't know."

"Look, I promise I won't tell anyone, okay? If you tell me how you play with people, then I'll tell you a secret, okay?"

"Deal."

"Deal."

He reached his hand back and she shook it.

"Okay. So you promised to tell me."

"Okay, but it's kind of gross."

"Shoot. I mean, tell me."

He could practically see Linda wrinkling her nose when she said, "Sometimes we have to eat people."

"Oh," John said. "That's not so bad. And this lets you play with people?"

"For a pretty long time. I don't have to eat the *whole* person. We all share. Mommy says we need to eat a person a month if we want to keep playing. She said if we don't, then we can't play, and then we might die except we're already dead and if we die then there's no place else to go so everything's just ... black."

"So what's it like?"

"Eating people?"

"Playing with their dreams."

"Well, after our feast, it's really easy. I can pretty much just close my eyes and do it anywhere. But it gets harder and harder."

"So what's it like?"

She didn't say anything for a while. There was only the sound of his feet on the road and his breath and heartbeat in his ears.

"Have you ever painted a room?" she asked.

"Of course," he said without stopping to think if he ever actually had or not.

"It's kind of like that. Like I close my eyes and open a door and there's an all white room and I make it pretty and funny. I don't have paintbrushes or paint or anything. Just my imagination and ..."

"Memories?"

"Are those like things that have happened to you?"

"Yeah. You know, when you say you *remember* something, those things you're remembering are called memories."

"Oh. Yes. Only when you're painting a room, you can only *see* what you're making. When I'm playing with people, I can *feel* what my imagination and memories are making them feel. That's why I like to imagine pretty and funny things. Because I don't like to feel bad."

"And some people *do* like to feel bad?"

"I guess. Or maybe they just can't help it. You'll have to try it sometime."

"Maybe."

They continued walking along and John thought about what she said. It seemed so chaotic. These spirits locked in this other world, living off humans that someone brought to them and, in turn, infiltrating the living's sleeping thoughts when their resistance was the lowest. But why? And who brought them the corpses?

"So why do you do this?"

"Because it's fun to play."

"I know that. But ... why do you play with people's dreams?

Aren't there other kids to play with and stuff?"

"There are but ... I wish mommy were around. She could tell you so much better."

"What would she say? What does she tell you?"

"She says it's how we stay in touch with the living."

"Maybe it's how you remember being alive?"

"Maybe."

"And the people you eat? Who brings them to you?"

She laughed. "People like you."

Then he laughed, again forced. "And what do you mean by that?"

"I know what you are. Not now, but sometimes."

"And what's that?"

She growled. "A *monster*."

"A *monster*?"

"Sometimes. I *know*. I can tell. You're not good at it yet, but you will be. You can make people like you or you can make them dead. And when you make them dead, we get them."

"I see."

"So now tell me *your* secret."

John took a deep breath. Where to begin, he thought. "Well, I've eaten people too. My parents."

She playfully smacked him on the back of the head. "That's *bad*."

"But it was an accident. I didn't know what I was doing."

"That's okay. Maybe they're here."

"Maybe."

"Maybe they're friends with Mommy."

"Maybe."

John was glad she didn't ask him any more questions. He didn't like talking about it.

"Linda?"

"*Yeeees?*"

"When you eat people, where do you go?"

"Where do we eat them?"

"Yeah. You said it was like a feast."

"We go to the church. That was weird at first because eating people seemed so evil."

"Could I go there now?"

"There wouldn't be anybody there. Besides, you're helping me look for Mommy."

They entered the graveyard and John felt a sense of complete hopelessness wash over him. Aside from the girl on his back, he felt burdened. Why was he here? What was he doing? Where was the girl's mom? Where was Ilya? Cassie? He needed to get back.

"You like it here?" Linda asked.

"I guess it's okay."

"Would you like to stay here all the time?"

"I don't think I can."

"You could. You could make it so we could all be together."

"Yeah? What do you mean?"

"I mean you could make it so me and Mommy could live with Daddy and Pete again. You could do it. I know you could. We've all been told about you. We've *all* been told about you."

John started to get a bad feeling about the girl on his back. He stopped and stood up straighter.

"Linda? I need you to get off now."

"Okay." She hopped off and, even though she wasn't that big, the relief was great.

She moved to his side and said, "Aren't they beautiful?"

He looked toward the woods. A number of grayish blue glowing figures came toward him. The number increased.

"Linda, I need to get back."

She giggled again. "We *all* need to get back, John."

Forty-three

Wayne felt out of options. After charging out of Melanie's house, he realized it wasn't a good idea to go running down the street so he ducked behind the house next door. He thought maybe running through people's yards was even worse. Growing up in the middle of nowhere could give a false sense of security about the ease of trying to find a place to hide. Until lately, he hadn't really had that need. Now it seemed like he was hiding from everyone.

He wished he had his phone.

Forty-four

Ilya didn't have time to take Melanie's car. She knew that would cause problems further down the road. She probably should have killed Cassie when she had the chance. Ilya had no idea who could have alerted the ambulance to Cassie's condition. Actually, she had an idea but it seemed absurd.

Hixon.

Had he followed her? She dismissed that thought almost before it had formed in its entirety. He was too stupid and lazy for that and he didn't have a car or a phone. But she was sure there were phones in Melanie's house. But why would he call emergency to go to John's house? It seemed pretty random. Unless he had more of the gift than she thought he did. She had bitten him as a slight precaution against this. She thought it would make him just disoriented enough to throw whatever it was that had led him to write that book out of balance. She mainly assumed he would lie around in a fog and wonder why he felt so strange.

Since she was close to the other house, she decided to go there. It would give her strength and focus. It wasn't hard to move through the woods unseen.

She made it to the house in a few minutes.

There was no sign of John anywhere and that was exactly as it should have been. He would be in Neverly right now. And he would be there until she joined him. He now had the ability to move back and forth between worlds. She'd given him that ability because it was something she needed. And he needed to be there alive. She could easily have sent him there dead like she had so many people but that wouldn't have benefitted her at all. In order to bring Neverly to Lynchville, John would have to die there. And after he died, they would take his body to the church and devour it.

She wondered what she should do.

She could keep Melanie's body, but it was possible people would be looking for her after they ran the plates on the cars at John's. And then they would notice there was a girl with a badly mauled neck and two missing people. The body was also a hindrance. She wanted Cassie dead. Maybe it was stupid and vindictive, but she wanted it to happen.

She sat and thought. Tried to clear everything else out of her head.

There were options, but they were getting fewer and fewer.

Forty-five

John turned to run, but Linda grabbed his hand and took him down. The others were upon him in a second. They were no longer so ghostly. They had gained substance. They lifted him up. He considered struggling but didn't see what the point of it was.

He felt panic but he tried to force it out of his head. He didn't know what good panicking would do. They were walking him back in the same direction he'd come from.

He tried to think of what the possibilities were.

Maybe he wasn't actually here at all. Maybe it was just a vision. That didn't necessarily mean it was any less dangerous but if his actual body was still back in that creepy house, then it was possible he could will his conscious mind or spirit self or whatever the hell it was back into his body.

Another possibility was that he belonged here. True, he was, at this point, being kept here against his will, but that didn't necessarily mean he wasn't here to do *some*thing. When he and Cassie had been stuck on the farm, that was entirely against their will but, by being there, they had prevented a far greater catastrophe.

So maybe he should just go along with it. These people probably knew way more about what they were doing than he did. He'd spent a few minutes with Linda and she didn't seem super evil. Of course, she had told him they eat people. But she hadn't said they eat people like him. She had said people like him brought the feasts here.

And that meant he didn't belong here, right?

In order to bring the living to them, he would have to be in the real world, wouldn't he?

They were now through the cemetery and headed back into town.

"Linda?" he said quietly, trying to crane his head around to see if he could see her. He didn't. He listened for her but, besides the sound of his breath and their shuffling footsteps, it was eerily quiet. He turned his head up to look at the blank night sky. He imagined himself sitting back in that old house. He imagined Melanie. Imagined biting her shoulder. That was when it had started.

Maybe this was just a nightmare brought on by guilt.

He tasted Melanie's blood on his tongue.

An unexpected vision popped into his head.

He saw Melanie in the old house, slumped against the same wall he'd passed out against.

He noted the rising and falling of her chest.

If she were not dead, then she shouldn't have been here. This was a place for the dead and the Devils, sometimes both.

He reminded himself that it was just his imagination, just a vision, just something he was seeing in his head, but he forced that away.

He let himself move closer and closer to the sleeping Melanie.

He drifted toward her forehead, looking for an expanse of smooth skin. Closer and closer until he didn't think he could go any farther.

It made him think of a door.

If he went through the door, he would either be in a room or outside. He wanted to explore either alternative. To explore inferred some form of control.

He imagined opening the door.

If this was a room, it was not a serene white room like Linda had said she encountered.

John immediately felt poisoned.

And that made him think of drinking Melanie's blood again.

A number of things flashed through his brain and he had to remind himself these thoughts were not in his brain. He was crawling through someone else's brain now.

Melanie's.

He saw himself towering above her down on her knees.

He felt himself inside of her, biting her.

He saw Cassie, bent over a table in front of him, a wine bottle shoved into her ass.

Then he saw another man. It was that guy he'd seen in the woods. The one who'd been shouting "Fuck" and chopping at trees. Then *that* guy was fucking her.

Through all of these encounters, he didn't detect a note of pleasure.

There was ... something else.

Something different than just *need* even. He certainly understood need. This made him think of something more akin to playing a board game.

He started to see other things.

Even more disturbing things.

A fat man, eviscerated in the woods.

A wasted looking girl, drowning in a pool of her own blood. No, not a pool. She was on a bed and the bed was soaked with her blood.

Something like ripples of interference disrupted his vision.

Maybe this person was waking up.

He wasn't sure what he should do.

If he stayed here, would he be able to control Melanie?

Only it didn't seem like it was Melanie at all. He couldn't imagine her doing those things, although she had admitted to leaving the offerings so maybe she was capable of more than he thought she was. A stabbing pain shot through him and everything went briefly black before he was fully aware of being in his body again.

He glanced to his side at the slouching buildings.

They'd entered town.

Forty-six

Wayne made it out of the suburb as quickly as possible. In Lynchville, things went from town to country pretty quickly. He crossed a country road and went into the cornfield on the side. He sat down heavily.

At first, he thought he was sweating like a pig and then he remembered that his clothes were wet when he put them on. Now they were damp and warm and heavy and maybe *they* were making him sweat like a pig.

His head swam around him.

He really didn't feel good. He would have blamed the scotch but he was sure his tolerance was higher than that. Especially with the good stuff. He was mostly used to drinking shit out of plastic bottles.

He wondered why he'd made that phone call. He wondered what the outcome would be. If there wasn't any truth behind the call, it was probably just another reason for the police to come looking for him. Only they'd probably be looking for whoever owned that house.

That made Wayne smile slightly.

But there had been a real moment of panic and concern when he was on the phone.

He thought about going to the hospital and finding out if they'd brought anyone in. If he had a phone, he could wait for a while and call. He imagined they would give him some vague amount of information.

From where he sat in the cornfield, he could still see the road. He thought about seeing Melanie pull past. Like she would pull past and instinctively know he was lurking there and then she'd stop the car and come and get him. He kind of liked her. He knew she was way too young for much to come of it, but he'd at least like to fuck her a couple more times. After all, the crime had already been committed.

He thought about going back to her house to wait for her but, if that call he'd made *did* turn out to be a prank, then he would surely get caught.

So that was out.

What was he doing?

Sitting here and wasting time again.

That was exactly what he told himself he wouldn't do. His mind was still open. He was still on the trail of the Devils. So he needed to go forward with his ideas, even the bad ones.

The only idea he'd had so far was checking the hospital.

The nearest hospital was on the outskirts of Dayton. Way too far to walk.

He stood up and began wandering back to the neighborhood. Even a passing car would do. He was already incredibly disheveled and looked like he'd sweated through his clothes. He lowered his head and clutched his heart, walked like he was in a lot of pain.

He hoped all the police were preoccupied with the emergency he phoned in.

He kept thinking somebody better stop quickly or he would be a goner until he reminded himself that he wasn't actually having a heart attack and, therefore, could walk around like this indefinitely.

His act must have been pretty good. The first car to pass him stopped. Wayne was hoping it would be Melanie, but it was just an old bald guy with a massive unibrow. He rolled down the passenger window and said, "Hey, chief, you okay?"

Wayne threw himself against the car, leaning his big, hairy head into the window. "I think I'm having a heart attack." Some drool came out when he spoke. "Can you call someone?"

The man was suddenly all wide-eyed concern. "If it's that bad, maybe I should just take you. Be quicker."

Wayne was already in the car.

Forty-seven

Ilya awoke with a start. She felt like she'd been invaded. Maybe it was panic or maybe it was something she'd decided beforehand, but she left Melanie's body as quickly as possible.

Suddenly, she floated over Lynchville, focusing on the ambulance in front of John's house.

She lowered herself, hoping to find the atmosphere mournful.

Instead, the EMT's were frantically working to keep the girl alive.

A cop was there, talking on the radio. He seemed to be asking about the call that brought the ambulance there.

"He said his name was what?"

A brief pause while the operator answered him.

The cop repeated: "Balls Ballserson?"

Then the ambulance was pulling away and flying down the country road.

Ilya pulled back.

She found a car heading down the intersecting road.

Suddenly she was in the driver's seat, her reflexes taking over. She looked into the passenger seat and saw Hixon having some kind of conniption fit.

She wondered what kind of mistake she'd made a second before she smashed into the ambulance.

Forty-eight

Wayne saw the ambulance pull into the intersection right in front of them, lights blaring. He briefly wondered if a person having a heart attack should shout, "Look out!" but it was too late. The car smashed into the ambulance, the driver's side taking most of the force. That was probably a good thing for Wayne. After breaking through the windshield with his head, it left him to fly unobstructed into a ditch on the other side of the road. His elbows took most of the shock and, before he could even think about what he was doing, he stood up and ran into the cornfield. He didn't make it very far before he collapsed into a shaking heap on the ground. It crossed his mind to wander back to the scene of the accident but he quickly dismissed that thought.

Forty-nine

When the car slammed into the ambulance, the back doors popped open and Cassie's gurney tipped over and slid halfway out. She was unconscious and had no idea any of this was happening.

Fifty

Tony Blevins was the name of the old man driving the car. He died upon impact. Ilya escaped his body the second before. A cop car was on its way. There was probably at least one more ambulance on the way, too. Ilya hovered above the cop car. She slipped into the one in the passenger seat. She wasn't going to let Cassie breathe through this. The cop car slid to a halt at the scene of the accident. The man driving said something but Ilya wasn't listening. She saw Cassie on the gurney, almost like she was propped there to provide a clean target.

Ilya stepped out of the car, withdrew the gun from the holster, and began shooting.

Again the man driving yelled something and then he pulled his gun and started shooting at Ilya.

She quickly left that body and hovered there just long enough to make sure Cassie had been hit. The front of the sheet covering her was red. That was good enough for Ilya.

She headed back to the house.

She needed to get to Neverly.

Fifty-one

Wayne heard the gunshots and staggered back to the scene of the accident.

He had no idea what had just happened.

An EMT stood talking to a cop. Talking was too tame a description. There was a lot of shouting and arm flapping. Wayne crossed the road, unseen behind the car he'd been riding in. He glanced toward the ambulance and saw a very bloody girl on the gurney. He wondered if this was who he'd called about. If this was who he'd "saved".

Before he could stop himself, he approached the gurney. He saw a dead cop lying on the road. He unstrapped the girl from the gurney and slung her over his shoulder.

He wasn't really that far from his house. He disappeared into the woods with the bleeding girl.

Fifty-two

John was so busy thinking about what he had just done that he was nearly unaware of what was happening to him.

He was sure he'd entered someone's thoughts and been kicked out when they had awoken. From what he saw there, he didn't think it was Melanie. Or maybe he just didn't *want* to think it was Melanie.

He'd seen her.

He'd entered her head.

Who else would it be besides Melanie?

Unless there was already someone else there.

He decided he wanted to try it again.

It was almost like he didn't care what was happening around him. If he'd been more aware, he would have noticed they had taken him into the church. According to Linda, this was where bad things happened. But he was convinced there were just too many of them and there wasn't any stopping what they were doing.

He closed his eyes again, imagined that house. No, more than imagined it. He made it real, closing out everything else around him. Felt himself drift into the house until he saw Melanie again.

And she was still there.

Still asleep.

No. Not asleep.

More like catatonic.

Her eyes were open but they stared straight ahead.

John wasn't sure if this would work or not.

What was he thinking?

He didn't know what the hell he was doing last time and didn't feel a whole lot more experienced now.

He just repeated the process. Moved closer and closer until he saw nothing but that expanse of forehead. Then he took a deep breath and *pushed*.

And then he knew what Linda meant by the white room. There wasn't anything here.

No thoughts. No images. No anything.

And when he opened his eyes, he looked through hers.

This felt almost like being in his world.

He reached into Melanie's pocket and discovered her phone. If he was here and able to use her body as some kind of puppet, then he could check on Cassie before returning back to that other place.

But maybe he *needed* to be there.

No. He needed to check on Cassie.

He tapped her name on Melanie's phone and let it ring. No one answered it. A voicemail prompt came up and he ended the call.

Maybe she was at his house.

He would check and, if she wasn't there, he would hope he could make it back to his own body.

Fifty-three

Ilya sensed what was happening in Neverly. It made her alternately happy and filled with panic.

They had John.

Now all she had to do was be there to finish the deed and the gateway between the two worlds would be open.

But she needed a body to go there. All the residents of Neverly, being dead, were uninhabitable. Maybe she'd been too hasty at the scene of the accident.

She swooped into the house and noticed Melanie was gone.

This filled her with even more alarm.

What if John had somehow inhabited Melanie and taken her back to Neverly to defend him.

Could he have learned things that quickly?

She thought he could. She'd been in Melanie the last time he'd entered. He shouldn't have known how to do that. It had taken her much training from her master. Of course, training was as much about *not doing* something stupid as much as it was about just knowing how to do something.

She needed a body quick.

And not surprisingly discovered Hixon walking through the woods with Cassie slung over his shoulder.

She hesitated before plunging into him. Knew that him becoming a hollowed out vegetable would only draw attention to him. Not to mention if she just abandoned his body in Neverly, which is what she'd like to do. But, maybe, since he'd drunk of her blood and was an idiot to begin with, the results wouldn't be the same.

She plunged in.

The initial thoughts were such a swirling morass of stupidity and filth she almost wanted to escape immediately.

She walked him back to that house. Dumped Cassie on the floor. Noticed the stupid bitch was still breathing. Now would have been the perfect time to finish her off but Ilya thought an author killing a teenage girl would have the same attention grabbing effects as an author going insane or an author disappearing.

Maybe it didn't matter. Cassie didn't seem in any condition to protect John anyway and, at this point, with the opening so imminent, maybe it didn't matter anyway.

Ilya closed her eyes, Wayne's eyes, and took herself to the church in the center of that beautiful, decaying town.

Fifty-four

Just the sight of this house filled John with an almost overwhelming sense of familiarity. It had been a very long time since he'd been away from it for this long. That familiarity was shattered when he opened the door. He nearly stepped into a pool of blood. There was more blood spattered around the living room and what little furniture there was was in disarray. Not smashed and tipped over or anything. Just not where he was used to seeing it. His first thought was that whoever had left the offerings had found him absent and decided to have fun with him.

But Melanie was the one most likely leaving the offerings and he was in her body right now.

That had only been for the past few minutes, though. Who knew what she'd been doing before, what?, taking a nap in that creepy abandoned house?

This was just rationalization. He was great at convincing himself of things and that was all this was. Him trying to convince himself the bloody chaos in his house didn't have anything to do with Cassie.

Deep down, he knew the chances were pretty good this *did* have something to do with Cassie.

He saw her phone lying on the ground and picked it up. He opened the text messages and scrolled through them, looking for some clue as to what might have brought her here. Most of the messages were just exchanges between her and Melanie. John felt himself grow angry until he remembered something horrible had probably happened to Melanie, too.

Still, the end result was that there weren't any easy answers and he needed to leave.

He wondered if it was as easy as closing his eyes.

He sat down on the couch and closed his eyes. He kept thinking of the blood, thinking of Cassie. Anxiety swarmed around him.

Concentration wasn't going to come here.

And maybe here was not where he needed to be anyway.

Quickly, he stood up and began walking back toward the abandoned house.

Fifty-five

Ilya slid into that other world with only a momentary lapse in consciousness and then a brief electric crackle. As always, it felt like coming home. Now she needed to get out of the woods and to the church as soon as possible. The person she was inhabiting was being remarkably quiet. She took off running and quickly realized this Hixon guy was wildly out of shape, but the basic genes were pretty good. He was a large guy and seemed like he had been muscular at one point in his life. So she just had to put the rasping lungs, throbbing liver, and stitch in her side out of her head.

She ran through the graveyard, through the streets, and burst through the doors of the church.

She was quickly restrained before being able to make it to the altar.

"Who are you?" Drew Benson asked.

"I am Ilya," she said.

"And who is Ilya?" Drew asked.

"I am the one who walks between worlds."

"And what is Ilya's purpose?"

"To make the worlds into one."

"And why should the worlds be made into one?"

"So it can be *our* world."

"You are Ilya. You may pass. The sacrifice is prepared."

The sight of John's body laid out and silent nearly took her breath away.

It felt like it should have been more ceremonial, but the Devils had never really been one for ceremony. Many of them had been here for a very long time. They just wanted out. For them, there was only this town. They were trapped.

And Ilya was partly responsible for that.

She slowly approached the altar. She saw the whole thing in her head. She wished she had been able to keep Melanie's body. It was so much like her original body. It would have looked so much better, the beautiful young woman bending over the powerful young man, biting down, not with the intent of turning but with the intent of killing, of draining the life from him.

If there had been any breaths in the room besides her own, there would have been a collective holding of them.

Toward the front of the group, a little girl looked at her. Her name was Linda Jennings. Ilya knew all of their names.

In a way, they were her reason for existence.

"Does this mean we can go home again?" Linda asked.

"Yes," Ilya said. She knew that wasn't exactly true. They could go back to Lynchville but, for a while anyway, it would feel like anything but home.

And what they would have to do to stay "alive" ... even though for them, life would be nothing more than existence.

Ilya bent over in the body of the hideous man she now inhabited. She smelled John's vitality. Smelled his power.

Now she knew why she'd made Hixon bite her that one night.

Even a small amount of her blood in his body was enough to forge a bond. It was enough of her to make her force his body toward something more like her.

She felt the fangs grow.

Felt the hunger well up.

She positioned her fangs against his jugular and flexed her jaws, heard the popping of skin and felt the rushing of blood.

And then she felt revulsion.

This was John's body, but John wasn't in there.

She lifted her bloody mouth and screamed.

The crowd began murmuring.

Fifty-six

John reached the other house. The decayed door already stood open. The first thing he saw when he walked in was Cassie, battered and bloody on the floor. Without even thinking, he dropped down beside her, lifting her head onto his lap. He stroked her bloody hair. Felt for the faint pulse in her neck.

Then it felt like he was yanked out of his body like a fish on a hook and he was back in that other place. Only his spirit flying through the woods and the cemetery and the town and then he was in the church.

The sight wasn't as disorienting as he thought it would have been. There was a group of the dead gathered around his body. That was pretty much the outcome he would have predicted when they were parading his body through the town.

The one thing he didn't understand was why that guy he'd seen in the woods was covered in his blood and shouting at everybody.

The force that John had felt pulling him toward this place was now trying to force him into his own body. Part of him thought he should have gone willingly, but a stronger part of him told him that he should get as far away from this place as he could.

"I know you're here!" the man shouted. "You could be responsible for a beautiful union. Don't you want our worlds to be joined? You could see your brother again. You could live the rest of your life protected."

John said nothing, but he didn't leave the church as quickly as he'd wanted to.

"Enter your body!" the man shouted. John knew this wasn't the man he'd seen in the woods. Not really. This was Ilya. A desperate Ilya so close to accomplishing what she'd worked probably hundreds of years toward. "If your body dies without the spirit, there will be no going back to that other world for you."

Still John didn't leave.

He spotted his brother Elliot in the crowd.

Watched Elliot become insubstantial and wink out.

John had his answer.

The man at the front of the church bent to drink the last of his life.

John turned to leave. He didn't know if he would go to the woods or the cemetery or any of the countless houses around here. He just knew he was going away.

Fifty-seven

Cassie felt like she was wrapped in a cloud. And it felt like the cloud was breathing around her. Slow and deep. But the breaths felt too far apart.

She couldn't remember anything that had happened to her.

There was just this now.

She felt like she should open her eyes. But she didn't want to. She wanted to stay in her cloud, her now.

She took a deep breath—

her last?

—and opened her eyes.

A man leaned over her and at first she thought it was John and then realized it wasn't. It was his brother, Elliot.

And she felt whatever was essentially her leaving her body and entering him. His mouth was fastened to hers.

She entered him and felt, horrifyingly, nothing.

It was like the complete opposite of her warm, safe cloud.

This was just black, empty space and she felt it to the core of her being.

Then ... life.

Roaring through her.

She opened her eyes again.

Again she saw Elliot over her, his mouth covering hers.

Then he stood up and was moving away.

Cassie sat up and looked down at herself.

At first she thought she was looking into a mirror and her heart did a wild, skipping dance in her chest.

She looked so bad. She looked dead. She reached out a hand and felt her neck on her lap.

No pulse.

This girl. This Cassie, was dead.

So who was she?

Slowly, she stood up and looked down at herself.

She recognized the clothes. She thought she would recognize that body anywhere.

Melanie.

Fifty-eight

Once the body in front of her was completely drained of life, Ilya considered using Hixon's bulky body to charge after John.

But that would have been pointless.

She slipped out of his body and floated high over Neverly.

She could see all the spirits, all the forms, everything.

He was in a house.

She went to him as fast as she possibly could.

Only here could she have the body she actually wanted. Her own. Sure it was only an archetype but the human physique was so ephemeral anyway ...

Fifty-nine

After waking from what had to be his worst blackout yet, Wayne decided he needed to get his life in order.

He stood in the front of the church with a mouth of blood. A dead boy lay on a sacrificial altar in front of him and there was a huge group of people wearing trashy, antiquated clothes staring at him. It felt like his soul had been raped but he didn't want to think too much about that right now.

"May I, uh, be excused?" he said. He didn't know who he was addressing. Not really. He was clearly in charge here. As if to affirm this, he shouted, "I'm in charge here!"

He parted the group of confused onlookers and stormed out of the church.

Sixty

John stood in Cassie's bedroom in the Neverly house feeling like he'd really fucked up. Maybe he'd kept Ilya from accomplishing what she wanted to accomplish but, really, what was the point. The Devils had existed probably as long as humankind. Their spirits had probably been contacting humans since then. So what if the doorway was opened? John was a Devil. Wouldn't that benefit him?

It would. That was the short answer.

But it wasn't just about him.

This was about being human.

It was what he'd been at one time.

After seeing Elliot, he knew Ilya had been wrong. John was not the only way to unite the worlds. Elliot could also travel between them. He'd come to Cassie before and John had rationalized it away as a vision.

He looked out the black and broken window.

A jagged hand of lightning flashed outside, almost hurting his eyes.

From behind him, John heard a soft voice say, "Now we finish."

Sixty-one

Wayne felt amazingly stoned.

Stoned and invincible.

He was barely aware of the decaying town around him or even where he was going. He would know when he got there. As far as he was concerned, his life began right now.

A thunderstorm seemed to be about ready to happen.

He liked storms.

Violent lightning streaked the sky and thunder rumbled deep and hungry.

Maybe he'd start a new book. That sounded like a really good idea. He could go back home and get a job at a bookstore or a bar or something.

A bar. That sounded like a great idea.

Rain began pouring down. He expected it to be cold but it felt warm. He liked it. He liked ... everything.

He became suddenly aware that he was smiling.

He couldn't remember the last time he'd smiled in a way that was not mocking or sarcastic.

Smiling like some kind of idiot lunatic, he wandered through the cemetery and the woods until he stood in that clearing.

It seemed like a good spot. A comfortable spot.

He felt like he'd made some big decisions in the last few minutes.

He was an atheist but he looked toward the sky and told the god he was almost certain wasn't there to strike him down if he was wrong.

The sky lit up with a skeleton of lightning so bright it made Wayne close his eyes.

When he opened them again he was in that creepy abandoned house.

Melanie stood in front of him looking at the dead girl Wayne had pulled from the ambulance.

She noticed Wayne and blinked her eyes. She looked dazed or maybe like she was in shock.

Wayne approached her, took her hand, and said, "Will you marry me?"

"I ... think I need to sort some things out. And I'm not sure I really know you."

"Fair enough," Wayne said. "I'm willing to wait."

Sixty-two

Ilya stood in the room, looking like she had the first time he'd seen her. She approached him. He considered lashing out or running away but didn't. He recognized something vulnerable in Ilya. Maybe it was some part of himself.

She put a cool hand on his cheek.

"Why do you fight something that could be so beautiful?"

"It's too late now anyway."

"But a time will come again."

"Is that what you want? Do you want to wait for that time to come again? Over and over? How much of your life has been spent waiting?"

She pulled back her hand. John felt like he'd spoken a truth and the truth made her flinch.

Now he put his hand on her cheek, slowly moved it down to her neck, and said, "Everyone I love is human. I'll do anything I can to protect them." He slowly wrapped his hand around her thin neck, almost expecting to find nothing substantial. Or that his own spirit hand would pass through. But it felt very real. They *both* felt very real. She continued to look at him, tears now streaming down her eyes, her pale face turning red.

A huge clap of thunder rattled through the old house.

"Do you know what you're doing?" she choked out.

John nodded and continued to squeeze.

The room lit up and flashed like a strobe light.

She began to weaken in his hand.

Wind hit the house, flinging warm rain into the room.

He smelled the tang of ozone from outside and wondered, "What am I doing?"

He held this woman in his hand and, for the first time, saw her as something other than a woman, something other than an evil being. Maybe she was a force of great destruction but she was also a force of great creativity. He remembered reading *Vampires in Devil Town* on the farm, making Cassie read it. He had fooled himself into thinking Ilya's story started there. But it went back further. Maybe even to the beginning of time.

And she was lonely.

He loosened his grip.

She coughed. Just a reaction. She didn't really need to.

Suddenly she was on him and he was accepting her and they fell to the bed and their archetypal bodies fell away.

The lightning reached for them, reached through them, became part of them.

John had no idea what was happening but he loved the feeling. He'd never felt anything like it.

Maybe it was sex but, without any bodies, it was hard to tell.

They swirled together and punched through one another like heavy oil paints fighting and combining.

At what was something like a climax, John lost all sense of himself. He could no longer tell where he was and where Ilya was. There was an explosion of thunder or something more chaotic and he opened his eyes to blackness.

Blackness and a stream of sorrow and heartbreak that reached back to the void.

And understanding.
He and Ilya were the same now.
And, together, they were Neverly.

Other Grindhouse Press Titles